MEDICINE
WHEEL

A Lizzy O'Malley Mystery

MEDICINE WHEEL

Kelly Running

Medicine Wheel

© 2013
Kelly Running

P.O. Box 1653
Lake Oswego, Oregon 97035

www.kellyrunningmysteries.com

ISBN: 978-0-692-63764-7

Cover and interior design by Indigo Editing & Publications.

To my sons

We walk in our moccasins upon the earth and beneath the sky as we travel on life's path of beauty. We will live a good life and reach an old age.

NAVAJO BLESSING

Contents

Chapter 1
The Argument

THE BLISTERING HEAT OF THE dry Arizona desert invaded the theater. Industrial fans buzzed to cool the dressing rooms, where actors were packed like wafers, waiting for the curtain call. Everything was ready to collapse under the weight of failed dreams. My brother and I were close to that point at the Sedona Theater.

"Lizzy," Ryan said to me. He was handsome and gay and in his midtwenties, and we were almost ready to start the rehearsal for *The Two Gentlemen of Verona*. "What do you think about an extra table or two over in that corner of the stage? And maybe some plants?"

Not ready for the opening performance next week, I had nervous butterflies. I lifted my bag off the chair, and it felt like a ton of dead weight. It was an occupational hazard as the stage manager. Screwdrivers, pliers, nails, hammer, plus the usual—wallet, keys—made my bag over fifteen pounds.

Last month Ryan had called and offered me the job as stage manager, but he hadn't mentioned Nicole Preston. I'd worked with her before at the Lakewood Center for the Arts in Lake Oswego, Oregon. Nicole loved party drugs, and when she was using, she was difficult.

I knocked on doors to let the actors know that we were about ready to start rehearsal. This was the last week of practice before we opened Shakespeare in the Courtyard. Actors looked over their shoulders as they descended toward the outdoor stage area. Tensions were running high in the desert-heat temperatures. Yesterday's rehearsal had ended with an outburst from Nicole. *What will happen today?*

The diva took a seat in a folding chair across from me wearing torn jeans and a loose-fitting T-shirt, though this was supposed to be a dress rehearsal. Her auburn hair was in a bun, and she wore beaded Tiffany-style earrings. On her feet were flip-flops. She also sported shocking-pink lipstick and an attitude.

She looked at Karma, my black Labrador, who was cast in the play. "Take Karma backstage," I said to Simon Barnard, who was sitting next to me. Simon was a heavyset actor with dark hair and a beard in full costume. He was a good-natured giant of a man who loved animals. Karma panted and fixed her gaze on some birds in a craggy tree by a courtyard fountain. I gave Simon some dog treats for the rehearsal and Karma's continued cooperation.

Twirling her hair, Nicole leaned over the back of her chair and said to me, "Dog's overweight." She popped a bubble of her gum in my face. "And Ryan's lost his touch. This shouldn't be the season opener."

I didn't have time for this. I still had props to buy and a background to paint before next week's opening. "Why don't you tell him that?" I said as I excused myself and went backstage with Simon and Karma.

Simon looked at me with sympathy. "Nicole could strip paint off a car."

I knew what he meant. Since it already felt over eighty degrees, I went to the courtyard office, once a greenhouse but now the center of the theater production, to get some iced water, juice, and soda.

Maybe some cold drinks will derail a tirade by Nicole? But when I returned to the stage, I found out I was too late. An argument had erupted between Ryan and Nicole.

"Can't this wait?" my brother said, his voice escalating. His neck veins bulged with tension.

Nicole waved her French-manicured fingers in his face. "No, it can't wait, because I can't live off a percentage of the receipts at zero percent. None of you can act, and you don't know how to direct a play." At that moment she lifted a stage prop, a terra-cotta vase, and threw it at my brother. Razor-sharp shards shattered on the cobble-stoned courtyard, missing him by only a few inches. He stood there, shaking. I moved toward her, but Nicole wasn't finished yet. She ran over and pushed my brother, hard enough that he lost his balance, and tumbled to the ground amongst the slivers of broken pottery.

He found his voice. "You're fired!" he yelled.

Nicole flipped him off as she stomped toward the Talaquepaque parking lot. The actors, momentarily stunned by the unplanned drama, applauded as Nicole disappeared.

We took a much-needed break. I decided to run an errand.

At a craft and novelty store, I loaded three fiberglass pots, two faux plants, and two ready-to-assemble side tables on a flat cart and pushed everything to a check-out stand. After paying, I wedged the items inside my car, like a puzzle. I needed to use my butt to shut the passenger door. The sun was high overhead, and it felt like it had reached the midnineties. As I pulled out, a traffic light changed, and although my first instinct was to run it, I made a decision not to. I passed the minutes by drumming my fingers on the steering wheel. I adjusted my air conditioning up to the maximum, which wasn't saying a whole lot in a car with over 125,000 miles on it. Faux fronds dangled in my face.

A Sedona police cruiser pulled up behind me. In my rearview mirror a police officer stared at me through his Polaroid sunglasses. I adjusted my mirror to get a better look at him. That's when I saw him flash the cruiser's lights. I pulled over to the curb. "License, registration, and insurance," he said as he stood outside my rolled-down window. His name badge read *Officer J. Hall.*

But in order to get the registration and insurance, I had to get out of the Subaru and open it from the passenger side and remove most of the faux fronds, fiberglass pots, and boxes with to-be-assembled tables.

When he came back, he handed me a ticket for a faulty brake light. No expression. It came back to me that my estranged, police-man husband had not signed the divorce papers to end our marriage. Emotionally, it had dissolved much earlier. It had something to do with the woman he was banging.

After he'd pulled away, I repacked all the props. Now I really was behind schedule.

Back at the courtyard theater, I set down one of the faux plants and handed my brother the receipt even though his hands were wrapped around his head.

I asked Simon to help me carry the rest of the props from my car. He agreed but first said to my brother, "Louise Smith can take the part." Apparently, they had been discussing a replacement for Nicole. My brother nodded as he swept pottery shards into a dustpan.

"Yes," I added, "a perfect idea." Louise Smith was a choice catch. She was on a summer internship and knew the part.

I smiled, but it occurred to me that the last time Nicole Preston had been let go from an acting job before, a suspicious fire occurred. Investigators determined that a flammable costume had been left too close to a portable heater and called it accidental. The buzz in the Oregon theater community was that Nicole had put her dress in front of the heater. The fire started in her dressing room.

I made the decision not to tell my brother. We needed a replacement. "Give Louise the part," I echoed.

My brother took a deep breath. "I'll tell Louise she's scheduled," he said. "I hope she agrees."

Relieved, I picked up the first items I'd carried with me—including a new Area 51 coffee mug—and went to the greenhouse office. My brother told me that the cast was at lunch at the Oak Creek Brewery and Grill, just a few doors down the cobblestoned courtyard from the theater. I decided to join them. Ryan declined because he planned to call and offer the part to Louise and had some other errands to take care of before the afternoon's rehearsal.

When I was almost done opening the boxes, I thought I heard someone in the costume room adjacent to the office. Maybe it was my brother? Maybe Simon made another trip from my car? I looked around.

"Simon?" I called out. "Ryan?" I waited.

There was no answer, but I felt an electric sensation throughout my body. When this happens it is not a good sign. My nerves under my left eye began to involuntarily twitch, a worse omen, and when I detected a faint metallic smell and all the hairs on my arms stood upright, it meant danger. I have some kind of sixth sense that goes off. Most of my life I have tried to ignore it. My Aunt Thelma, a psychic, wanted to teach me about it, but I never cooperated.

My breathing quickened. But when I didn't hear anything, or see anything, or feel anything else, for at least five minutes, I let it go. I locked the office. Under the sun's heat again, I took the alley toward the Oak Creek Brewery and Grill, up the Spanish-style steps to the second level. The cast was at an oversized booth looking at a courtyard fountain. Two pitchers of amber ale sat on the table. Jake Jordan handed me a glass.

"You found us," he said. "We ordered burgers—want one?"

"Yes." I was starving. I hadn't eaten anything since last night.

"Oh my god," exclaimed Megan Kennedy, dangerously exotic and equally dramatic, "I've never seen anything like that argument with your brother. Has he figured out who will replace Nicole for the opening?"

"He's going to ask Louise Smith."

Conversation was postponed when the Oak Creek burgers with mounds of seasoned French fries, fried pickles, and ranch dip came to the table.

"Hey," I said to Simon after I'd finished my meal, "did you go back to the greenhouse after that first trip when you helped me?"

"No," he said.

"Oh. I thought I heard someone in the costume area." *I'm going to get that side door fixed.* I'd put some heavy props in front of an unused side door until I could get a replacement lock. The door was overgrown with vines on the outside, but I worried that someone might see an entrance and come into the greenhouse office through the costume room. Now that the theater was active, we had expensive props and costumes stored there.

Simon added, "We didn't get paid today."

All the actors were on an hourly rate except for Nicole. She'd negotiated a percentage of the receipts—and that fed into her tirade today.

"I'll talk to my brother," I said. "He must have forgotten."

"Lizzy," Simon said, "I've rent due tomorrow."

When I got back to my studio apartment in West Sedona in the late afternoon, I was still troubled by the sensation in the greenhouse. I called my Aunt Thelma, who had raised me in my tumultuous teenage years. If anyone could help with sixth-sense experience, it was her. She lived in an assisted living center—she'd been diagnosed with moderate dementia, though most of the relatives thought Thelma had been crazy all her life. My call almost went into voice mail but then she answered, "Hello, Lizzy."

I sighed in relief. *Thank goodness. She remembers me.* We talked for a bit about her apartment at the assisted living center. Then I brought up the sensation at the greenhouse.

"It was a spirit guide," she said without hesitation. "I sensed something universal this morning. I've sent you white light. Give me your address."

I recited my latest *temporary* address in what appeared to emerge as a pattern in my life. As if she read my mind she said, "I'll draw a cup of tea and read the leaves—and let you know if any messages come through." She promptly hung up the telephone.

Chapter 2

Navajo Artist

ON THE DAY I MET Ellie Chavez, a Navajo native with raven-colored hair and dark eyes, a jewelry artist by trade, I had the day off from the theater and had gone to a jewelry and craft fair near Tlaquepaque. I didn't have anything specific to buy—maybe a souvenir for Aunt Thelma who believed in any kind of amulet. The day smelled of barbeque mixed with the scents of cinnamon-sugar sprinkled fry bread and hot corn greased with butter. The sky was a brilliant azure, and the russet clay of the earth radiated heat.

Chavez's booth stood out with sapphire-blue, red, and orange-russet gems and crystals, as well as silver jewelry crafted by tribes in the area. Chavez, seated behind the counter, suggested I pass my hand over the raw stones. She calibrated my hand over a large stone, and when I felt some kind of energy, she told me to pass my fingertips over the other stones. Eventually I selected a turquoise amulet swirled with brown minerals, which caused a tingling sensation as my hand hovered over the rock.

I decided to get something to eat and drink before the crowds overwhelmed me. I found a booth that sold fresh-squeezed lemonade and a food trailer that served barbequed chicken and roasted corn with melted jalapeño butter, and I reveled in the explosion of flavors—that's when I saw Chavez again. Her braided raven hair contrasted exquisitely against her latte-colored skin. She sat down opposite me. I admired her handcrafted turquoise-and-silver bracelet.

I have a passion for jewelry. Southwest jewelry is a favorite of mine, like the Hopi's designs that are overlaid with stones. Navajo jewelry is typified by repetition and balance—something that energy vortexes in Sedona are famous for. Symmetrical designs identify a piece as Navajo. Then there are the Zuni who make fetish necklaces—strands of tiny animals carved from stone or shell.

I found myself back at her jewelry booth. I'd walked away earlier from the expensive pieces, but I was drawn back to the bracelets as if I were in a trance. I pointed to an exquisite piece of Southwest turquoise under locked glass, tooled in silver in a wide-band bracelet. The silver was etched with a beaded design and embedded with large chunks of turquoise, but the fabulous part of the design was the large, dark-veined, blue-green turquoise stone in the center, which had come from an Arizona mine.

"Fifteen hundred dollars," she said. "It's worth twice that amount. It's a collector's piece."

"Who made it?"

"It's made by a special Navajo jeweler who sells exclusively to me. It's one of a kind, and I've had several people who are interested in it today."

It was as if she had read my mind. I couldn't let such a treasure go to anyone. I had to have it. It didn't matter that the amount represented my entire savings account.

She rang up my purchase, handed the card back to me, and said, "Is there anything else?"

I looked at the new bracelet on my wrist.

"No, thank you," I said.

I was ashamed when I got back in my apartment and clipped on Karma's leash. We were headed toward a park. *What am I doing?* I'd succumbed to a jewelry purchase as a way to get over my pending divorce. Now the guilt would follow—just like the credit card bill.

Chapter 3

Opening Night

I WAS AT THE THEATER kiosk for the opening performance wearing my turquoise and silver bracelet. It looked exquisite on my tanned wrist. The outdoor work in Sedona had made my skin dark. My reddish-brown hair had summer highlights from the sun.

My brother arrived. "New jewelry?" he asked as he noticed my bracelet. He knew about my appetite for it.

I wrinkled my brow. "Some things don't change."

"You deserve someone in your life who can afford to buy you these kinds of things," he said with a gentle smile. "You've had a bad year," he added with unconditional love. He'd arrived with a date—someone I hadn't met before—but he didn't take the time to introduce him. *Must be a lot on his mind with opening night.* I didn't press it with Ryan because someone was approaching me for tickets. The line grew longer. I'd just sold the last ticket for tonight's opening and was finished putting the last of the cash and receipts in a metal strongbox when I was surprised by two uniformed police officers. I recognized one of them as the police officer who had given me the ticket earlier in the week. As he stood leaning on the kiosk counter, I shook off my momentary infatuation with him.

"Where's Mr. Ryan O'Malley?" he asked me. I was surprised, but I pointed toward the greenhouse office.

What do they want? I thought as I watched them disappear into the office. I was about to take the cash box to my brother when he appeared—now with hands behind him, handcuffed and led by the two officers.

"Nicole's been murdered!" he yelled to me as they marched him past the kiosk. He had wild, stunned eyes. I watched as the officers directed him toward the police car parked in a tow-away zone by the stage.

"Help me," my brother called to me as Officer J. Hall assisted him into the back of the police cruiser. Waiting patrons, tickets in hand, turned toward me for an explanation. I didn't have one.

"I will!" I called back to my brother. As the cruiser pulled away, puffs of dust floated in the warm air and shadows flickered off stucco walls of the businesses surrounding the courtyard theater.

My brother's date ran toward the parking lot.

I'd spent a good part of the evening at the police station after the performance but gotten nowhere, so I'd gone to bed, exhausted, and temporarily out of ideas. In spite of my brother's arrest, the opening performance had gone well. I hoped the *Sedona Red Rock News*, Sedona's local newspaper, had more details. I found a short article in the crime blurbs:

Shakespeare Theater CEO Charged with Death of Actress

Sedona—The CEO and managing director of the Sedona
Shakespearean Festival, Mr. Ryan O'Malley, 25, was charged
with murder in the death of 21-year-old Nicole Preston, who
had worked as an actress at the theater. Hikers found her body
at the Wallow Canyon Trail Vortex, a hiking destination.
Sedona Police Department Cmdr. T. J. Barnes reported that
O'Malley was taken into custody without incident and is
being held at the Sedona Detention Center.

I looked at the byline. The article was written by Hugh Rossi.
That's serendipitous. Hugh and I had dated. I'd met him shortly after
I came to work at the theater when he came to write an article about the
theater's reopening. After the interview he asked me out. I explained
to him that I was still married—although separated. He insisted we
go out to dinner. After our third date, I told him I wasn't ready for
a relationship. Now, since I planned to pop back into his life, I decided
the best use of my time was to take some kind of peace offering with
me. I changed into khaki shorts and a fuchsia shirt. I twisted my auburn hair into a French knot and put on my silver loop earrings along
with a little makeup and left for the newspaper office.

When I entered the main lobby of the *Sedona Red Rock News*
and asked for Hugh Rossi, the receptionist pointed toward a cubicle.
The woman gave me a precisely plucked eyebrow arch, like I was
one of many who came looking for Hugh. I followed her finger to
the cubicle where Hugh Rossi worked in front of his laptop computer, which formed a tiny respite from the open architecture of the
newsroom. I waved a vanilla latte at him like a peace offering, and
he groaned with pleasure.

"You didn't return my calls," he said with a bit of a pout, "but this makes up for it."

I pulled out a mint-chocolate brownie and handed it to him.

"Marry me," he said, impulsively.

"Not on your life," I answered with a laugh. "Besides, I'm still married."

"Not for long," he said as he took a bite of the brownie. "Isn't your hotshot attorney fast-tracking the divorce?"

"No attorney works like that."

Hugh was married for two years, and it ended with a quickie, do-it-yourself divorce. He caught my glance, sipped the latte, and furrowed his eyebrows. "Legal stuff got you down?"

"Yes," I answered.

"Is there anything I can do?"

"Can you help me help my brother?" I felt butterflies in my stomach.

"The police think they have a pretty good case. Sorry to hear he's been charged with it. Cops have been very tight-lipped. I was about to drive out to the crime scene because I heard, through a source and off the record, that her body was discovered with burning sage in a newly constructed medicine wheel. The killer stuffed her mouth full of pillow stuffing— to shut her up for good."

He leaned in and added, "Did you know there was another murder a year ago by a medicine wheel? Sedona cops never arrested anyone. They don't want that to happen again."

Hugh called up the newspaper articles from that time period on his computer. We read that over the course of a week, the newspaper had reported daily information about the killing of Jane Corbett, twenty-two years old and single. The chief of police vowed to solve it, but after extensive interviews and time spent, no solid leads came forth. The breaking news story described how the victim was found by a tourist hiker. A Forest Service representative spoke about the conflict between the National Forest Service and the New Agers/Vortex Lovers. The Forest Service worked to preserve the area as pristine, given the number of people who made pilgrimages to the vortex sites, and citations were issued to anyone who was caught constructing a medicine wheel in the National Forest.

By this time Hugh and I had spent an hour on the computer. Hugh looked at me with a satisfied grin. I suggested that we print out the remaining articles and head to the vortex.

Once at the trailhead, Hugh set an easy hiking pace. The trail narrowed as we came to a flat expanse of red rock and the remnants of a medicine wheel. Hugh took out a notebook and pen and lowered himself to examine the stones. "I know you haven't lived here long," he began, "so stop me if you know this. When people come to the medicine wheel, they often bring sage for smudging. It's used for cleansing. People use the smoke to create a place of peace and healing. It amplifies any intentions."

"I didn't know you believed in mysticism," I said. "I thought you were more of a spring-training baseball kind of guy."

Hugh laughed. "You're correct about the baseball," he said. "I had the sports beat for five years. Then the newspaper transferred me to religion and art. When I complained, my editor told me to either take it or leave the newspaper, so I decided to connect to my spiritual side."

"What kind of person would hurt someone at a medicine wheel?"

Hugh's eyes were dark. "Maybe someone integrated into the community, someone without suspicion, someone Nicole knew and trusted. And Lizzy, has it occurred to you that your brother may have killed her? They had a very public argument."

I was surprised that Hugh knew about it. He shrugged when he saw my expression. "It's a small town, Lizzy. Word about bad mojo travels fast around these parts."

"My brother didn't kill Nicole, and I have to help him. I know that public defenders will want him to plead guilty and cut a deal. Most don't even try to find the truth."

The view toward the western ridge was filled with blue sky and red rock. At any other time, I would have found it stunning. Now I was beginning to withdraw into myself and couldn't distinguish much of the color in front of me.

"West is the ability to look within for answers," Hugh said, looking at me with compassion. "State your intention facing west like it already happened."

I stopped and inhaled deeply. My tear ducts were damp. Toward the western red-rock canyon with the manzanita and dark niches I said, "The crime is solved. My brother is free."

Hugh gave me some cornmeal to sprinkle on the earth.

"Now," I said, "let's get to work and explore the crime scene."

"Are you up for this?"

I had to do something. I had to make an *attempt* to help my brother. "Yes," I answered with more conviction than I felt.

Hugh pulled out his notebook and started to sketch the wheel on the pages. "I'm counting the rocks," he explained as he drew. "Usually sixteen to twenty rocks form the large circle and it contains the universe—all things, people, animals, the rocks, wind, are in a relationship within it. A smaller circle in the center, as this one has, are the four directions—east, west, north, and south. Each stone contains an intention to the earth."

"What do the other directions mean?"

"North is the gift of wisdom; south is trust; east is illumination— seeing clearly. Each direction has a color and a totem animal. This vortex accesses past memory and future memory along a timeline."

Finding nothing at the scene after another hour, we hiked back down the trail. I didn't expect to find anything today, but I was disappointed nonetheless. Hugh explained that he had a deadline for an article and dropped me off in the parking lot of the newspaper.

I drove back home and picked up Karma from my apartment. I planned to go to the office and find Nicole Preston's phone number and residence on her employment application. It was the only other thing I could think of to do. I also intended to visit my brother at the jail in a few days if bail wasn't posted, but I didn't know where I'd get the money for bail. The theater needed to continue to have good receipts. My brother had used his inheritance savings for a down payment to purchase the theater earlier in the spring. He had called me and asked my opinion. I'd told him it was a good opportunity for him to have his own business and make a name for himself as a director in the acting community. My brother's problem, however, was that he wasn't always good at picking the best people to hire. Nicole was an example.

It didn't take long to find the employment application for Nicole. Scanning the file, I read that she lived in the city of Cottonwood. Cottonwood was about sixteen miles south of Sedona on I-17. I reasoned that I'd be cutting it close before ticket sales, but if I went now I might be able to talk to some of Nicole's neighbors. Getting ready to write down the address, I pulled out the desk drawer to find a pen, but I was distracted when I heard something rolling in the drawer. I looked behind a stack of papers and found a prescription bottle. I paused. Oxycodone. And the prescription bottle didn't have my brother's name on it. I put the bottle neatly back in the drawer. I sighed. My brother had a problem with prescription drugs in the past. I hoped that it had stayed in the past.

Looking at my watch, I knew it was time to get moving. What was going to be tight had gotten even tighter. I hurried outside, turned around, and bumped headfirst into a reporter from the *Sedona Red Rock News*. Hugh had introduced us before. She worked the arts section of the newspaper.

"Rebecca Fuller," she said, extending her hand and rubbing her head.

"Lizzy O'Malley," I answered and shook her hand. "Sorry about that. I was pretty distracted."

"No problem," she answered and added, "The murder of the lead actress is tragic."

Rebecca Fuller's hair was streaked with heavy blonde highlights. Her nose turned up a little, and she wore jeans and a light blue cotton see-through blouse. Underneath she wore a lace camisole. I could tell she wasn't here to offer her condolences.

"I'll be writing a review after tonight's performance," she said.

This could be a deal-breaker for the theater. I'd done my best at making the sets and costumes. We needed good receipts. I was ready to give some positive quotes about the theater, but she preempted me when she asked, "Who replaced Nicole Preston for the lead?" She whipped out her reporter's pad.

A little caught off guard, I answered. "Louise Smith. She's brilliant."

Rebecca's response startled me. It wasn't about the theater. This had been a ruse for her visit. She said, "He's quite the stud, Hugh. I guess you know that since you were his date de jour last month."

Rebecca Fuller had her sights on Hugh. She felt the challenge. My time with him today did not bode well for the theater.

"Hugh and I are just friends," I said.

"Good," she snapped. "Keep it that way."

The interview was apparently over. She turned her back toward me and walked away.

I knew that Cottonwood, Arizona, had an early history of lawlessness. Bootleggers lived in Cottonwood in the past, and more recently another vice came: crystal meth. With the Mexico border not far away, heavy drugs were part of Cottonwood. I was without a clear idea of what I'd do, but I had to do something for my brother. He would do the same for me.

When I found it, the apartment had a look of neglect. Paint peeled off the whitewashed exterior. Shutters, once proudly hung from the windows, tipped like drunks. I pulled into the parking lot where two men washed a decrepit Chevy and consumed conspicuous amounts of beer. With Karma, I walked over to the alcohol-chugging men. I approached with a smile and tried to be friendly. I started the conversation with a lie. "My friend was Nicole Preston," I said. "She used to live here. Did you know her?"

Both looked at me blankly. "She was about my size and weight," I went on, "and I think she lived in that one." I pointed to a second story unit, number 204.

"You're not the type we see around here," one of the men said when he finally got a voice.

The one with greasy hair in a ponytail belched. "She was crazy and sexy. She'd dance for us. You gonna dance for us, too?"

"No. Because she's dead," I said. "Murdered. And I don't dance."

The other one turned toward me. Half his teeth were missing. He had the sunken cheeks of a meth user.

"She had a boyfriend," he said with a sideways smile. "He's not going to be too happy about this."

"Bitch was always high," the other added. "Boyfriend got high, too."

"Cops talk to either of you?"

"Nah," greasy-hair said, "We've been across the border." He gave a sidewise glance to his friend.

"I bet you could learn to dance for us," the other one pressed. "Want some beer? Some shots? I've got tequila in my apartment. Want something to make you feel more like dancing?"

"The boyfriend's name?" I persisted. Greasy-hair shrugged his shoulders.

"Do you know where the boyfriend lives?" I pressed.

"Might tell you if you move your hips around. Like a hula girl."

Karma growled.

"You got yourself a mean-ass dog?" he quipped.

The other greaseball pointed north toward Sedona with his beer, spilling it down his hand and legs. I don't think he cared if I danced. "Boyfriend worked for that company with the pink Jeeps."

The other took two steps toward me and said, "Now how about a little kiss…"

Karma's hackles went up. Her teeth bared. Greaseball backed off a few steps. "Lady, take your dog and get. We didn't mean any harm. Just havin' some fun with you, you know?"

I turned around and steeled myself toward the apartment with Karma. When I tried the front door, I found it was broken off its hinges and had been leaned back into place. Very little furniture filled Nicole's last living space, which was stifling hot—a faded green couch under the only window in the living room, which had dis-eased-looking drapes, one side hanging precariously on a bent rod. In the bathroom, the cabinet had several empty prescription bottles.

The air was even denser in the bedroom, and it smelled like dust and cigarette smoke. I opened an accordion-style vinyl closet door. A few outfits hung in there. Black slacks, white blouses that needed bleach, and an iron. Karma started to growl. I looked at her, and then, I, too, heard soft footsteps and heavy breathing. A burning metallic taste filled my mouth. I grabbed a lamp. Karma barked, teeth showing. She was ready to leap on grease-man's throat when he came through the bedroom door. I was about to let go of Karma's leash. He sensed it and backed away from me.

I counted to twenty. I couldn't hear any heavy breathing any-more, and the hairs on my arms had returned to normal. No more metallic taste in my mouth. It was time to get out. Karma and I walked through the apartment living room, past the faded couch and stifling heat. I looked out the open front door. The two men were gone from the parking lot. By the time I was on the highway, my knees and arms started shaking.

Karma wagged her tail.

Chapter 4
Looking for Clues

THE NEXT DAY, I DROVE to the main office of Jeep Tours, an icon of the tourist industry in Sedona. Inside, a sandy-haired man with a soul patch on his chin handed me a flyer for the Jeep tours. Bulletin board pictures displayed smiling happy customers. Bags on the counter held sage and sweet grass. I sniffed through the plastic. A hand-printed sign said that it was for peace and healing.

"I want a tour," I said after examining the brochure.

"Indian ruins or a vortex?"

"What's the tour that Dave Lewis drives?" I asked. That was the name on the prescription vials that I'd found empty in Nicole's apartment.

"He drives the Indian ruins tonight at six o'clock."

Bingo. I was on to something. "Make it for two people and a dog."

He wrote the reservation in a book. "Be here about ten minutes early."

I called Hugh when I was outside. The heat spiraled in mirages off the hot pavement. "Will you go with me on a pink Jeep tour of the Indian ruins? I have a clue." Hugh had offered to help me since he wanted a new lead on the case. He thought if he could break this story open, he would have a shot at a promotion. I also thought I needed some help after I'd been to Nicole's apartment.

"I knew you'd crush under my charms," Hugh said and laughed.

"This is work," I said as I thought of Rebecca Fuller's review in the newspaper. "Meet me at the main office of Jeep Tours just before six o'clock tonight. I really need your investigative prowess."

"Don't you have a show to put on?"

"The theater is closed Monday nights. This is one of the times I can do it."

"Okay, then. My reporter's instinct knows we'll also need a bottle of wine, some soft cheese, like a Brie, and fruit and chocolate."

"We're on the trail for clues," I insisted, "not romance."

"I never heard a rule that one is exclusive of the other," he answered.

Now I have even more to worry about.

I showered, changed into something a little more casual, and got into the Outback with Karma for the drive back to Jeep Tours. Hugh pulled up minutes later. Only one person was in the office. He wore a blue denim shirt with the business logo on the front and his name, Dave, embroidered underneath. His eyes were black and rat-like. So this was Nicole's boyfriend—the one who may have weaseled his way into both Nicole's and Ryan's lives. We exchanged pleasantries. He was nervously tapping his pen and then pointed to the parking lot, specifically to a neon-pink Jeep.

"Let's go," he said. Not one for small talk. "Another couple cancelled," he said over his shoulder, "so it's the three of us."

"Where should I put this?" Hugh asked about his backpack.

Dave opened the latch of the Jeep cargo door and pointed toward the mesh cargo hold. Hugh placed the backpack in it and used a bungee cord to secure it.

"Hop in," Dave said. Then he looked at me and asked, "Have we met before?"

"Never," I said.

He shrugged.

We climbed into the passenger seats, which consisted of two benches facing each other. Karma hopped on her own bench. Hugh and I sat behind the driver's side. It smelled like gym sweat and dust. We turned onto Highway 89A. As Dave drove, Hugh peppered him with questions about baseball—Arizona Diamondbacks, batting averages, and free agents.

Karma sniffed out the open side of the Jeep, drooling down the side of it.

Soon we were off the paved highway and on the rock-crusted road. It was about a twenty-minute ride through the landscape of the Coconino Forest—agave, prickly pear cactus, pine, and juniper. When we finally stopped, I'd quit listening to both of them. Karma jumped out to pee by a bush. I clipped on her leash.

Dave led the way. In the heavy gray of twilight, as I hiked behind Hugh, I found myself thinking back to the day that I found my husband and his sleep-around girlfriend together. It was about a year ago, and I'd just finished working at a theater class at a community center. We lived in a modest house in Portland that we'd mortgaged up to the maximum. I'd poured my father's inheritance money into it—both for the down payment and the money for renovating it. We worked on it together—me with the color and design, painting and buying fabric to re-cover flea market furniture—he with the hammer and nails remodeling the bathroom, replacing tile with the flavor of old Portland.

I'd just picked up some fresh strawberries for dinner at the farmer's market and saw a car I didn't recognize in the driveway. It seemed unusual, but I didn't spend much time thinking about it. I unlocked the door and called out to him.

No answer.

That's when I heard a muffle and a whisper. When I reached our bedroom, my white Egyptian sheets were wrapped around four legs. One set of the legs belonged to a woman with huge breasts swaying over the top of my husband's face. My timing was impeccable. My husband convulsed in climax, big-boobs groaned in pleasure, and I dumped the strawberries on them.

He was lucky I didn't shoot them both on the spot. Especially since his service Glock 23 was next to both of them on the nightstand.

Dave finally stopped at a clearing he used for his guide's spiel. We found a place to sit on some large boulders. Karma sat down on her haunches and panted. Dave took a small box of wooden matches and a sage wand out of his pocket. He struck the side of the matchbox and flame danced from the tip. Bending down over the sage, he lit it. The sweet aroma spiraled upward. He said it was important to smudge with sage before we took the trail to the Indian ruins. He tried to sound like a spiritual leader. He said that we might see some of the spirits that lived in the rock at the ruins. I figured if I drank that bottle of wine with Hugh later tonight, I might see some of them, too. I brought the smoke to my face and rubbed my hands in it. Hugh stood and did the same.

"I'm sorry about your girlfriend," I said offhandedly to Dave.

He stopped the smudging in midair. "You knew my girlfriend?" he asked with worry etched across his face. He didn't act like someone who'd had a loved one murdered. He acted more like someone who had a lot to hide.

"We worked together at the theater," I answered.

He put down the sage wand. "You here for the tour or to ask questions?" he asked as his rat-eyes got even beadier.

Before Hugh or I could answer that question, Karma growled. I told her to sit and tried to ignore her. I didn't want Dave to stop talking now. But it didn't matter because Karma jumped to her feet and bolted, pulling the leash right out of my hand.

"Karma," I hollered. "Here!"

She bounded up the trail toward the Indian ruins as the canyon exploded with gunshots. I called out again to Karma, panic rising. Gunshots didn't bother her well-bred hunting instincts. But when I heard a bullet fly over my left ear, Hugh, Dave, and I hit the ground.

I gagged on dirt. *Oh, no. What can I do?* Unreasonably, I stood up to go get my dog. Hugh pulled me back and told me to stay put. Bullets flew, hitting cacti and ricocheting from rocks.

"We're completely vulnerable—stay low and head toward the Jeep," Hugh said. We slithered through red rock and cacti, the earth still warm from the day's sun. I saw Arizona bark scorpions dashing under rocks. Another hail of bullets reminded me that scorpions were the least of my worries. My clothes were torn and my skin bloody, too.

"Where's Dave?" I asked looking over my shoulder breathlessly when I'd made it back to the Jeep.

"He was behind me. Then he disappeared."

The Jeep was without a key and without a guide. I turned toward the wheel wells to protect myself. Maybe, I figured, if a tour guide lost his key, there might be a contingency plan. I didn't have any other ideas, so I fished my hand up into the wheel well. Nothing.

I slithered to the next tire and repeated the process. Hugh crouched down low and got to the other side of the Jeep. He shook his head when he hadn't found anything. I decided to try the front grill. There was just enough room for a key box. My hands shimmied into a small crevice on the left side, and it came back—with nothing. Panic set in as I heard a bullet hit the Jeep bumper. I fished my other hand into the passenger side of the front grill and felt something. Hugh looked at me with hope. I extracted a magnetic key box, slid the cover sideways, and saw a Jeep key.

Hugh jumped in the driver's seat, and I jumped into the passenger side. I stuck the key into the ignition, and Hugh turned it. It started! Bullets continued to pound the Jeep. By this time rich twilight had descended and the sunset, well past, cast evening into dark shadows.

"I'm steering by moonlight," he said as he accelerated and took off into the desert, loose rocks flying from spinning tires. *Ping. Ping.* I heard the Jeep hit again and again.

Once we were clear of the shooter, our troubles were not over. The Jeep weaved crazily. We stopped to examine our surroundings and the Jeep. We needed a plan. There was no road. We were on an animal path, deep in the desert. Looking over the damage to the Jeep, bullets had entered and exited. The Jeep's back tire was flat. We regretfully decided to keep going, riding on the rim, since neither one of us could get a signal for our cell phones and we didn't have a better plan.

Maybe Hugh was good at driving in near pitch-darkness, I consoled myself after I agreed, but I observed beads of perspiration forming on his forehead. Added to that, lightening sheared the sky as a big storm loomed. Thunder growled. *Kaboom.* I counted. *One, one thousand, two, one thousand.*

"So, who's trying to kill us?" Hugh asked me. Worried wrinkles crossed his face.

"I don't know," I answered.

Large drops of rain had splashed on the windshield, mixing with red-rock grit to create an opaque mess. That's when the cold sensation encapsulated me. Hugh turned on the wipers, but we couldn't see anything in front of us. Terrified by the onset of a strong premonition, I shouted for Hugh to stop the Jeep. But before he could put on the brakes, gravity had taken over, and the Jeep was airborne, in flight, over the edge of a cliff.

Chapter 5
Lost

"HUGH," I GROANED. NO ANSWER. Through the window, upside down in the Jeep, I saw blue sky and turkey vultures circling. Something had died. I looked over next to me. Hugh was still strapped in his seatbelt; the driver's side had taken most of the impact. I reached over and felt his neck for a pulse. Nothing. Hugh was dead.

I had to get out of the Jeep. I released the seatbelt that held me to the bucket seat and fell toward what was once the roof. I slid out and walked. I was ready to vomit.

I was in a canyon, in early daylight, stretching for miles in every direction with no civilization in sight. I knew I couldn't leave the way we'd come. It was too steep. I shielded my eyes from the rising sun. My right arm throbbed from pain. *Must be broken.* I walked back toward the Jeep to see if I could find some water. Even an empty water bottle would be better than nothing. I dropped my head back into the Jeep, looked around, and found a half bottle of water and a granola bar. I put both into my pockets. I couldn't find the backpack that had been in the back. *Must have flown out of the Jeep before we hit bottom? Or did Hugh have it with him?* I couldn't remember.

The Jeep was crushed like an aluminum can, and I had to walk out. Prickly pear cactus dotted the landscape. *If I can find a road or highway*, I reasoned, *I can flag down a motorist for help*. But also present in my mind was the worry that the shooter would come back to finish the job. *Did he see the crushed Jeep at the bottom of the canyon and figure it's over? Now will the desert kill me?* Hope entered my thoughts when I thought about my absence at rehearsal this morning. *Surely someone will question my absence and look for me, and won't the same questions arise when Hugh fails to show up?*

I stopped dead in my tracks.

Am I dreaming, or is there someone out on the distant horizon, and is it someone I want to see? He looked to be male, twenty-something, medium build, wearing jeans and a short-sleeve shirt—I couldn't make out his face since I was too far away. Or was it a mirage? No truck, no vehicle. He was sitting there, with some shade from a piñon pine, not making any kind of movement. I hid behind manzanita and watched. The only time I moved was to find some shade. The minutes ticked by. Insects ran across the hot sandstone like water droplets dancing on a hot skillet. I traced the path of the sun and figured it to be getting on toward three o'clock. Hell, I was hot, tired, and my arm hurt. And I couldn't stay out in this bleeding desert forever.

I needed a plan.

Clouds rolled in toward the canyon. The change in weather gave me some shade, but I kept undercover and edged slowly toward the cliff, now hiding behind the larger rocks. I hugged the cliff wall to put distance between us. After some searching, I found a larger niche where I could hide. I curled into a fetal position on the shelf cliff and thought about a day ago when I was in Sedona, surrounded by potable water and friends.

Night fell. I listened to the heavy rain as I watched from my cliffside niche. The howl of the wind sounded like voices across the desert. That's when a ghostly white form appeared to me. It looked like my Aunt Thelma, but I knew it couldn't be. I wracked my mind to remember if I'd read about end-of-life experiences like this.

My aunt, or rather what appeared to be my aunt, advanced toward me as if she could see me. *But she lives in an assisted living center in Portland.* I blinked, rubbed my eyes, and figured I might be dead and not know it. But even with that thought, the figure clearly became my aunt—my fragile, ninety-year-old aunt. I moved my arm, and it wracked me with pain. I knew if it hurt that much, I was still alive.

"I don't know the way back!" I yelled at this apparition, and huge sobs welled up into my chest. "I'm hurt."

My aunt's spirit stood above me while torrents of rain fell. She walked a few steps from the cliff face and, taking a branch from a nearby pine, dug a slight hole in the desert sand. It didn't take long for it to fill with the rain water, and I remembered the story of how the cliff-dwelling people were able to farm in the desert by planting corn in this kind of circle, so the rain would collect and nourish it. It came back to me so clearly now; I didn't know why I hadn't thought of it sooner. I worked through the pain and felt for my empty water bottle as I crawled like a snake toward the circle. I drank deeply and then filled the bottle again. I worked my way back the way I had come. Before I lost consciousness, my aunt turned, looked at me, and walked back into the dark night. I wanted her to stay with me, but the pain won out and I drifted back to the comfort of darkness.

When I woke up again, she was there. It was early morning, and the chill brought me back to life. By my hand was the half-filled bottle of water. *I'm not dreaming.* It had rained and I had gathered water. My clothes were covered with a thin coating of mud where I had slid toward it.

This time my aunt beckoned me to follow her. I didn't know how I would be able to do that, but I found my legs. With rest and water, I was able to move. It amazed me how agile she was at her age, stepping through the desert with confident steps. And so I followed. When I'd call to her to slow down so I could catch up, she kept the same amount of distance from me. In this way we went for some time, until I had to find shade in a small cluster of pines and juniper. I sat and looked around me, exhausted. Everywhere I looked, it was the same—blue sky, red rock, and desert. I looked again toward my aunt, but she had vanished. I curled into a ball and fell asleep in the afternoon heat.

By the time I woke up again, the sun had set and the day had started to cool, and it would soon be dark. I waited for her to appear. I didn't know if I was lucid, but without any other options, I worked on faith. The stars had come out—bright in the sky without any other lights—when she appeared before me. This time she was fully formed and beckoned me to follow her with her hand. I was rested and ready. That's when, to my amazement, her form began to glow and she transformed in front of me into a silver-gray owl that circled and plunged and then flew toward a distant light in the desert that I hadn't seen before. I thought of the owl as a totem, and I watched as my aunt transformed herself. The gray feathers flashed silver in the moonlight. I confidently followed. Her wings shone as a beacon. I trusted this spirit. As I approached the light, I saw a fire, and the silver owl descended to the shoulder of a Navajo elder with glistening russet skin wrapped in a blanket and gazing at the cliff's overhang.

"Sit," he said. "I've been waiting." He stirred something in a container over the fire, poured it into a cup, and passed it toward me. "Drink."

I took several sips from the cup—something I'd never tasted before—and could feel my pain abating.

I was able to say in a hoarse voice, "I'm hurt and lost and my friend is dead."

Whatever he'd given me to ease the pain made me see double. My eyelids dipped. I tried to shake it off but couldn't. The elder Indian sat like stone until he began to swirl and change shape. He grew larger, darker, and his skin turned darker brown. In front of me was a gigantic brown bear, swimming in a golden aura.

Chapter 6
The Navajo

I WOKE UP IN THE back of a pickup bed, jostled by the driving. I looked up at the blue sky and tried to remember what had happened to me. I propped myself up to peek into the cab of the truck. A man with a mane of raven-black hair, pushed by the wind in every direction, was driving. I ducked down into the truck bed, pretending to be unconscious while I figured out my options. I really didn't have any except to wait and see where he was taking me.

The jostling finally ended. I heard the man get out of the truck and the door slam shut. His boots crunched on the gravel under his feet. I listened as his steps approached me and the tailgate popped down. I kept my eyes shut, still pretending to be out. A blanket under me lifted, and what surprised me was the gentleness with which I was carried. I was placed on something solid, and when I heard the footsteps fade like they were in another room, I opened my eyes. Around me was a small bedroom, clean but sparse. The sun shone through a window from the upper part of the room. That was the only window, and since it was a tiny thing, I knew that I couldn't get out through it.

It was quiet. I tried to turn over and put my feet on the floor. Then I attempted to put some weight on them. That seemed okay, so I stood, but when I felt an explosion of pain in the balls of my feet, I cried out. I was about to topple over onto the floor when the man walked into the room, silently and swiftly, and nimbly caught me, preventing my fall.

He scooped me up into his arm like I weighed just a few pounds, which I most definitely did not, and carried me into a living-kitchen area, where he placed me firmly in a chair at a Formica table with a swirl pattern in the gray surface.

He smiled. "I see you're awake."

I had a difficult time keeping my eyes off his mane of black hair and rugged features. He seemed to be able to read my mind and threw back his head in a laugh. I felt my face turn red, and that seemed to please him even more. "Color in the cheeks," he said, "another good sign." He turned to the sink and filled a glass with water to the top. "Sip on that."

I took the glass into my hand and tried to drink and swallow. I was satisfied that I could still do something so basic. He walked over to a coffee pot and filled it, carefully pouring the water from the carafe into the coffee maker. He opened a canister of coffee and scooped the grounds into a filter. He flipped the switch on the coffeepot, and within minutes the room was filled with the aroma of fresh coffee.

I can't be dreaming this, I thought. *It would be too cruel.*

He went over to a small refrigerator. It was an old-fashioned, rounded model of late years and only about five feet tall, probably from the '50s. He opened it with a click of the handle and took out eggs and meat along with a bottle of orange juice. He looked over at me in a nonthreatening way—almost like he was talking to himself—and said, "We're going to start with coffee and see how that settles and then try the food."

He worked to thinly slice the meat—paper thin. "I thought, at a distance, you were a ghost, but then I heard you talking to spirits."

Up to this point, I wasn't sure if I could talk, but the water had eased the constriction of my dry throat. I tried to say something, but only a croak came out.

He didn't turn around, but kept at the preparation at hand—pouring some oil in the bottom of a frying pan and placing the thinly sliced meat into it. When joined with the oil, it made a delectable sizzle, and the aroma wafted through the room, and I realized that moisture was returning to my still parched mouth.

He cracked the eggs into another pan he had greased on the back burner of the two-burner gas stove and poured two cups of dark coffee, one of which he set in front of me before he went back to work at the stove, drinking coffee and carefully placing a spatula under the eggs. "I'll make these fairly well-done," he said. "Better that way with the buffalo."

He whisked the eggs and meat out of the pans and put the food in front of me. My mouth salivated. I don't recall the sensation of hunger, but when I smelled the food, my stomach reminded me that I was—starving, actually. I remembered the last time I'd seen food, and that led to my horror-stricken recollection about Hugh.

"What?" the man asked.

Struggling to find my voice, I explained the crash that had killed Hugh.

The man listened with sympathy and said, "You're on the Navajo Reservation. I found you about two miles from here. Amazing, quite frankly, you're not dead."

The Navajo Reservation was north of Sedona.

He must have sensed my next question and gestured toward my sling. "I put that on you."

My arm didn't hurt so much anymore.

"Don't think it's broken. Swelling is down." He grinned and added, "But you look a little like a lobster with that sunburn."

I was confounded with the thought of what I looked like—*ugh*.

"Eat something and clean up," he said. I followed his gaze to a bathroom. "Clean towels over the shower. Water would feel good, maybe."

I took a few bites then excused myself and limped into the tiny bathroom. There was a mirror hanging over the sink, and I stoically examined my reflection. Tiny blisters covered my face. I looked like hell. I peeled off my dust-covered and torn clothes—jeans that I remembered freshly laundered the evening I'd met Hugh at the tour office. My sleeveless white blouse was torn and covered with dried blood. Turning on the water in the shower stall, I was careful to direct the water flow toward parts of my body that didn't hurt. Fairly successful, I lathered up and rinsed off. I splashed water on my face, arms, and legs.

I got out of the shower and with a towel in hand patted off the rest of me and looked down at my clothes. I was ready to put on the jeans and blouse again when I heard the man's voice through the door: "Clean jeans and shirt by the door."

I took a towel, covered myself, and opened the door a small crack. I looked down at the floor and saw the clothes. Everything was too large, but I rolled up the jeans and the sleeves on the shirt. I smelled the scent of detergent. Walking out of the bathroom, I went back to the kitchen table and my food was still there. I tried a few more bites. The man stood at the sink, washing his plate, shaking the rinse water from it, and placing it in the drying rack on the counter. He went back to the coffeemaker, refilled his mug and mine, turned the chair around, and sat down across from me.

I could tell he was ready to ask me something, but he was interrupted by the sound of a vehicle engine and tires. He stood up, walked out the door, and disappeared. The vehicle stopped. I heard an exchange between the parties—although I had no idea what was said, it sounded like Navajo. Then I heard: "She's inside."

I'm not sure what I expected, but this is what I saw: In front of me was the elder Indian I'd seen in the desert. My face must have shown my amazement, but he didn't show any recognition of me, and before I said anything about it, there were introductions.

"I'm Kuruk," said the old Indian.

"And I'm Danny."

"I'm Lizzy," I said.

"Let's start with some coffee," Danny suggested.

I explained everything that had happened. I even explained the part about how my aunt had turned into a silver-gray owl. I was ready for Danny and Kuruk to tell me I was crazy. Instead, Danny turned to Kuruk and said, "I'll get the truck."

"Where are we going?" I asked.

"To visit some friends. Are you up for it?"

"I'm an old man," Kuruk answered, "too old for chasing around." He looked at me intently with piercing eyes. "Listen to the spirits," he said, "iPhones, laptops, email—they compete with spirit messages."

"Don't scare her," Danny said.

Kuruk smiled. "Enough talk from an old Indian."

I rode in Danny's Ford Ranger. I felt a peaceful balance that I hadn't felt before. He stopped at a small store off the highway. Before he got back in the cab of the truck, he asked if I wanted anything. I declined.

43

When he got back in the truck, he had a newspaper tucked in his jeans back pocket, and he passed an icy-cold Coke to me.

"Now," he said, "Let's go see those friends." Miles of desert loomed on all sides of us. While Danny was driving, I looked at his key chain. It held the emblem of the Cleveland Indians.

"That's not politically correct," I said.

"That's why I have it," he answered and grinned.

Danny took a turn toward a side road marked with a mile post and desert brush. After endless dust and cacti passed, we stopped at a hogan. An old dog came over and paced around Danny's truck.

"Hello, Zeek," he said as he got out of the Ranger. The dog sat and waited. Danny put his hand into his pocket and pulled out a dog treat. Zeek stood up on his legs in a celebratory dance, and Danny patted him on the head.

I thought about Karma. Danny was at my side in an instant. "You lost all your color," he said in an attempt to explain why he had his thick, muscled arms around me. "I thought you might keel over."

A woman came out of the house and a smile swept over her face. "Welcome, Danny." Then she looked at me. "You brought company." Looking slightly embarrassed, he released me, but not too quickly.

"I'm Lynea." She had a light complexion with long black hair. She wore it pulled back to the nape of her neck and braided. She was dressed in jeans with a sky-blue tank top and wore layers of silver and turquoise jewelry—tooled silver bracelets—at least ten on one arm. Silver earrings were fastened in symmetry along the curve of her ear.

Lynea said, "Rudy will be back late this afternoon. He'll be disappointed he missed you."

Over a meal, I learned that Lynea was Danny's sister-in-law. Rudy, her partner, had a counseling job on the reservation. Lynea worked at the reservation school, now on summer break.

"I need to tell her," Danny finally said to Lynea.

"Tell me what?" I asked, sensing something dark.

"Tell her about Kuruk."

"Kuruk came to us about a vision. When you know there's trouble on the horizon, is it better to know or not to know?"

"Can Kuruk tell what this trouble is?" I asked.

Danny took the *Sedona Red Rock News* out from the back of his pocket and spread it on the table. The headline jumped out at me and I whimpered: *Sedona Red Rock Reporter Dead.*

"Kuruk knew about this before it happened. And he knew about you."

Chapter 7
Navajo Medicine Man

I SCANNED THE ARTICLE IN the newspaper. "This is awful," I said. "The police want to talk to *me*."

"Earlier today, you were lost," Danny reminded me.

"It was with Danny's help and Kuruk's vision that you are alive," Lynea said to console me.

A thought occurred to me. "There isn't anything in the newspaper article about the guide, Dave Lewis." I explained to Danny and Lynea how he'd mysteriously disappeared when Hugh and I were dodging bullets. "I wonder if there's more to it."

Lynea came over and put an arm around me. "Let's go cleanse to interpret the vision," Lynea said. "Sweat lodge cleansing is how the Navajo people see clearly. Anglos in the sweat lodge are rare, but Kuruk knows you are central to the vision he has seen. He drove ahead this morning and made the preparations. He's waiting for us."

A Navajo medicine man waiting for me. *Will cleansing in a sweat lodge give me the insight and vision I need to help my brother? Will I be able to interpret Kuruk's vision through the ancient rites of the*

Navajo? And if spirits are communicating with me, what will happen if I don't take the time to listen?

Danny drove us farther into the reservation until we stopped at a small hogan. He promised he'd be back for us by evening. The sweat lodge was located yards behind the hogan and was made of split cedar, arched in a dome. In front of the sweat lodge was a burning fire. It was there that Kuruk greeted us. The sun was beginning to set as he prodded the hot rocks. When he was sure they were hot enough, he took a pitchfork and set them in the sweat lodge. Lynea explained to me that Kuruk would put these in the north corner to ward off any evil wind that might try to enter the lodge.

Lynea led the way through the blanket-covered door. It was completely dark inside. We sat down on the ground, covered in bark. The rocks warmed the sweat lodge. Kuruk poured water on the stones. The water vapor filled the lodge and the Navajo medicine man's song began.

Lynea had told me that there were four songs that Kuruk would chant. Afterward, we would leave the lodge and enter again—followed by four more chants from him.

Since I couldn't see much except the glowing rock, I found my other senses working in overdrive. The melodic singing of Kuruk felt otherworldly. Lynea whispered that he was summoning the earth, wind, and fire. After the first chant, he threw more water on the stones. The smell of piñon pine and juniper engulfed the lodge, and I soon found myself unable to concentrate on any words.

I was walking with Kuruk, no longer in the lodge, but out in the bright daylight. I asked him, "Why have we left the sweat lodge?"

Kuruk turned to me and said, "I'm in the lodge. Your spirit is dream traveling. Follow it. It will lead you."

Kuruk and I walked along the canyons of the reservation, covering much distance with little effort. We saw a small herd of javelina along the way. "They look like pigs," I said of the salt-and-pepper mammals that scurried away from me. We also saw mule deer and cottontail rabbits, quick and fast.

We traveled across vast areas of the desert in short amounts of time, and I marveled at the agave with the yellow flowers at the top of long stalks signaling the final days of the plant's life. There were fuzzy cholla cactus in bloom and the saguaro cactus. We moved without effort around manzanita and ocotillo until we both stood over the canyon where I'd plunged over the edge in the Jeep. From this perspective, I was amazed that I'd survived. Then we were at the bottom of the canyon, near the crushed Jeep. I turned and remembered the figure in the desert where I'd seen it before. This time I recognized the face—it was Danny.

"His spirit helped to guide me."

Kuruk nodded.

"And my aunt's spirit is here," I said and pointed. In the distance the gray-white owl descended, its wings in silent flight.

"My aunt is watching," I said. "But a danger is present."

Kuruk nodded again.

Another spirit came toward us, approaching cautiously in the form of a great buck mule deer. I recognized him. "Hugh, are you okay? I vow I'll find out who did this to you." The mule deer turned, and I watched as it bounded off into the north, the direction of the white buffalo and winter.

"Goodbye," I called after him.

I was in the sweat lodge again, and Kuruk had finished.

Outside with Lynea, I heard him sing in Navajo. Lynea explained that he was singing a prayer of thanks to the spirits of the sweat lodge and the Blessing Way song as an apology for any mistakes he may have made.

Danny parked the Ranger next to the hogan and walked over to us. "Ready to get some dinner?" he asked.

"Is Kuruk coming?"

The medicine man appeared from the sweat lodge. He looked a little more hunched over than he had this morning. Danny went to him and spoke in Navajo. He came back and told us that Kuruk wasn't going to join us tonight.

The medicine man waved goodbye under starlight.

At Danny's place we ate grilled mushroom corncakes, sweet potato crisps, and marinated bean salad. The main course was roasted corn and golden tomato pasta. Lynea talked about teaching on the reservation. Rudy explained his work as a counselor helping Navajos with employment skills.

And just when I thought I couldn't eat or drink anymore, Danny brought out the dessert—chocolate and raspberry sorbet.

After the final course, we went out into the desert evening and watched the parade of constellations move across the western sky.

"Danny plans a healing for you tomorrow," Lynea said before she left with Rudy. I watched as a puff of dust left a trail behind their four-wheel drive.

Danny asked after they left, "Do you want to watch more of the star show?"

"Yes," I said.

We climbed into the back of his Ranger, lined with blankets, his arm around me, and watched the desert night sky.

I woke in Danny's hogan with a pillow under my head, wrapped in blankets, sunlight blazing, with the smell of strong coffee. I opened my eyes to find Danny standing before me with a broad smile on his face.

"Kuruk gave us a day off today, so let's look for your dog," Danny said.

I hugged him.

Chapter 8

Finding Karma

WE DROVE THE HIGHWAY SOUTH then veered east and exited the highway and traveled dirt roads. *What are the odds of finding her?* I thought. I was in awe that I'd managed to come out alive—the crash, the desert—what were the odds? I knew someone wanted me out of the way.

We searched in vain for hours for Karma. Finally, when we were hot and tired and unable to go any further, we stopped at a café. No sooner had I sat down than Danny got up and said he'd be back for me in a little while. He wanted to drive into Sedona and see if Karma had shown up. I wanted to join him, but he overruled it. He was sure someone was still trying to hurt me.

Danny drove off down the highway toward Sedona. The waitress came over and asked if I wanted coffee. I did. I looked over the menu and ordered a turkey sandwich, but after it came, I picked at the food until the waitress came over again and offered me a box to go. She brought my change. I counted out a tip. Danny had given me twenty dollars. I looked at a pay phone across the parking lot, and I took my leftover sandwich. I listened for the dial tone. I knew this number by heart.

"Law office of Jake O'Brien, divorce specialist," said a voice that I recognized as his legal assistant.

"This is Elizabeth O'Malley," I said. "I need to talk to Mr. O'Brien, please."

I heard, "One minute," and listened to the automated music. Then I heard a click.

"Elizabeth," I heard him say in that formal way attorneys like to talk, "I've been worried about you. You didn't return my calls."

I told him about my brother's arrest, the accident, Hugh's death, and my short time with the Navajo.

"I urge you to go to the Sedona police as soon as possible. They will want to question you, of course. If you need an attorney present—"

"No, I'm not ready to go back yet," I interrupted.

Since he wasn't making any headway with me on that issue, he updated me about the divorce. "Opposing counsel returned my telephone calls," he said with a hint of frustration in his voice, "and your husband's retirement account is an issue. They'd like for you to consider letting him keep all his retirement assets."

Retirement assets. He'd worked for the police force for five years. "If he keeps his retirement, then I'd get an equal amount from the proceeds from the house sale?"

"Of course, that's what we'd counter with, but I had to speak with you first."

"Fine," I said. "Let's do it."

"I'll call opposing counsel, and if agreed, I'll draft a revision of the proposed settlement. Is there somewhere I could fax it to you if we get his signature?"

"You could send it to my apartment address."

"I'll call opposing counsel now."

"Thanks, Jake. I appreciate everything."

"Elizabeth…"

"Yes, Jake."

"Callaghan asked about you."

Oh. My uncle—the only remaining connection my brother and I had to that nebulous part of the family, and a powerhouse Portland attorney.

"I'll try to call him," I said, not sure that I would, or what I'd say if I did, or why he wanted to connect with me now when he'd so graciously disregarded Ryan and me before.

"He wants to talk. People change. I believe he's sorry for the way he's treated both of you."

"I'll think about it," I said.

I saw the Ranger turn into the parking lot as I walked out of the telephone booth. "Good news," Danny said to me. "Karma found her way back to your apartment a day ago. She was hungry and thirsty, but otherwise, she's fine. An actor named Simon is keeping her. Dog's still in the play; the joke is she couldn't miss time on stage—she has acting in her blood. I told him you were okay. Everyone was worried about you."

Chapter 9

Healing

A SPIRIT RETRIEVAL, OR SOUL retrieval, is where a medicine man or shaman travels into the spirit world and assists in taking back what belongs to the person it originally came from. The other person can't use the spirit—it's like excess baggage—but it makes the person who doesn't have it incomplete. Signs of soul or spirit loss occur if a person has trouble moving on from an issue or if there has been great hurt involved—kind of like the brain going into a coma to protect itself if there has been great trauma to the body.

It's dangerous for a medicine man to travel into the spirit world to help retrieve the spirit. Not to be taken lightly, it would be work for me, too.

Danny had offered the healing, and I'd accepted. Ready to begin the ceremony, he called upon the spirits of each direction for their help—each with a totem and each with a spirit guide. Once he'd evoked the spirits, he placed his hands on my neck and shoulders. My eyes had been covered with a bandana that smelled of sweet grass. I'd been smudged with sage for cleansing.

He had me breathe in fully and exhale deeply. Through the rhythm of my breathing, I heard the Navajo words in the present moment, but my spirit traveled to retrieve the missing pieces. I intensely wanted them back. No blame here. I had allowed myself to give these fragments of myself away, and now it was like running a marathon to retrieve them.

I could see what I'd lost—it was a vision coming to me, and I called to it to come back. And then I saw the people who had hurt me in the past. Danny encouraged me to keep at it, not to give up, to keep breathing, and he journeyed with me to make me whole again.

I shed my wedding dress at the edge of a cliff. I was able to jump over a deep canyon—and I was on the other side. I could see that I was once again on my true path. Danny was there to encourage me as well as Kuruk and my aunt. My animal totems joined me.

And then I heard the words of Danny as he thanked the spirits of the east, west, north, and south and the spirit guides for their help.

"It is done. You need to eat lightly today and sleep."

It's hard to explain what happens with a soul retrieval healing, but I knew, without a doubt, that I was Lizzy again—still very aware of the memories of everything that had happened to me, but complete, and whole, and intact.

I slept most of the day.

When I got up, Danny was reading a book. "Do you want something to eat?" he asked.

"Sure," I said.

We went to the kitchen, where I sliced some fruit and cheese. Danny opened a bottle of wine. We arranged it on a tray to take outside into the early haze of twilight. It was about seven thirty, and it would be dark by eight. We sat and ate. My spirit was whole, although still exhausted from the healing, and I looked upon the stars, and the desert, and Danny with a clearness of vision that was unparalleled. I could *really* taste the grapes and the strawberries—the tangy bouquet of life.

Danny said, "I discovered I have healing medicine power. I'd denied my father's way of life for so long. I came back to the reservation to find what I was missing. Now I'm back for good."

"What did you do before?"

"I was in the military. Lived in California," he said. With that, the Arizona night lit up with a shooting star.

"That's a good sign." I took his hand in mine. The purple desert sky and the icy-white stars were reminders of life. We started to kiss. Before I knew it, we were in the hogan, eager for each other. However, by the early hours of the morning we were nestled in the confines of the sun-kissed quilts while we took our time—sensual and deliberate with each other.

When the morning sun shone through the windows into Danny's bed, he and I had quilts wrapped around our legs and bodies. I'd slept with such innocence that when I heard a knock on Danny's hogan door, I was startled. Danny kissed me and brushed a strand of hair off my face.

He got up and went to the door. I recognized Lynea's voice.

Danny came back into the room and took me in his arms. Lynea had been sent by Kuruk, and we were to meet at the sweat lodge at one o'clock.

Danny kissed me again. "Sweat lodge after we have a few more hours together."

After some effort, we showered, had breakfast, and were en route to the sweat lodge. We pulled up, and Kuruk had the ceremonial fire burning, even larger than before. We could hear Kuruk's sweet melodic Navajo voice chanting.

"Powerful medicine," Danny said.

Danny and Kuruk carried the hot stones with metal tongs into the sweat lodge, and I followed. As before, the heat in the hogan was intense, and this time Kuruk poured something scented with the essence of cedar on the stones. He passed around a hollowed-out wooden cup. Each of us took a drink from it, and then we passed it around one more time. I immediately felt a tingling sensation, and then dizziness took over, and I saw Kuruk and Danny outside their bodies. There we were, all three of us on the red-earth floor of the sweat lodge, our spirits hovering above ourselves.

I heard Danny say, "Kuruk said to me: Spirits can travel together." Danny's spirit took my hand, and we soared over the reservation and over the Coconino Forest.

"This is where I first saw your spirit. I heard your call for help," Danny said.

We were above the desert again, over the agave and the prickly pear cactus and the manzanita, and then we were at the niche where my aunt's spirit first appeared to me. The great, gray owl flew down upon us without a sound.

"What is it, Aunt Thelma?" I asked the winged spirit.

In front of me, Danny's spirit turned into a majestic, sleek black raven, and he took flight with the gray owl as Kuruk and I watched. They soared high above the desert out of sight.

But the black raven returned and retransformed into Danny's spirit. "I promised I'd look after you. She doesn't have the power any longer."

And once again we were hovering over the crushed remains of the Jeep. At the top of the canyon cliff, I saw the perspective of the crash. Clearly, some hand of fate had kept me alive.

We stood at the top of the butte and a great buck came to us. It stood in front of Kuruk's and Danny's spirits. Kuruk transformed and ran with the buck toward the west. When we looked again, only Kuruk's spirit returned.

"I traveled north for a great distance with the spirit. He sees danger, even from far away," Kuruk added.

Continuing, we came to a shelter by the Indian ruins. It was toward the red-rock brick wall that the cliff dwellers had constructed eons ago—two levels of living—and there Danny, Kuruk, and I approached the ruins.

One ancient spirit came forward and reached his hand out to me. I took the ancient's hand, and I saw myself in the shelter below the ruins with Hugh's spirit. But what I hadn't seen from this perspective was the danger in the cliffs west of the ruins, where two men held rifles.

I watched as they tracked us until they got to the edge of the butte. The three men argued; they looked over the edge of the cliff at where the Jeep had plunged.

And then a dark spirit appeared on the horizon. The wind blew with force, and the darkness settled. In the distance, I saw a swirling, dark cloud as it hovered over Tlaquepaque.

I recognized Nicole's spirit. She was a ghostly apparition.

She was caught between worlds. Out came a wail that was not of this world. But I held to my compassion, and she looked at me in her ghostly form and pleaded with sunken eyes.

And with that, the apparition faded.

I was back in the sweat lodge with Kuruk and Danny. Inhaling the cedar, sage, and sweet grass, I was in my body again. As before, I left the lodge and we heard Kuruk chant the Blessing Way song.

When Kuruk emerged from the lodge, he looked at both of us with a deep furrow in his brow.

Chapter 10

Relationship

DANNY AND I AGREED TO spend Mondays together since I had the day off. Danny wanted to protect me all the time, but I pointed out that no relationship could withstand that kind of smothering and that we both had jobs, so we compromised. We agreed that we were only a call away from each other, and I had to get back to my life and find a way to help my brother.

He made me promise I wouldn't do anything impulsive. I agreed. Of course, I never did anything with that kind of intent—it was always after the fact that I'd seen it for what it was, but I decided I wouldn't mention that to Danny since we seemed to be on a good roll as far as compromising goes.

My plan was to get into the greenhouse office for more information from the personnel files. The theater was plugging along—actually, the receipts were good, a packed house every night—since the whole murder of Nicole and a missing stage manager had the public's interest. The theater had almost a cult following now, showing up to see what would happen next—on or off stage.

Danny made me promise that I wouldn't go after Dave Lewis and his greaseball friends alone. I agreed to that, thinking about the moment in Nicole's apartment. Something else worried me, and I couldn't get my mind around it. Maybe it was the peyote that kept me in a haze or maybe it was the residual effects of almost dying in the desert. I wasn't sure.

I also didn't mention this to Danny, because he was in a protective mode that men get into. Danny and I were engaged in a collective dance of compromise. I knew the police would take up an inordinate amount of time with questions. But I also knew that facing them was inevitable when I showed up in Sedona. I hoped for a little time.

Since I knew it wouldn't be too long before the Sedona police buzzed around me, I decided to try to get some inside help from Rebecca Fuller. She could move around the community without much notice in her job, and I needed her help.

Danny and I were at my apartment, but I didn't have my key anymore. I had one of those apartment doors that can be opened with a stiff plastic credit card. I asked Danny for one of his, and without much effort, the door popped open. Danny rolled his eyes, but I told him I had an inside dead bolt lock that I promised to use whenever I was inside.

He had his arms around me before the door clicked closed, and it wasn't passion that drove him. He advanced into the apartment, pulling back drapes, looking out the living room widow, and searching the other rooms to make sure there wasn't anyone inside. The good news was that no one had decided to break and enter—the bad news was that I didn't know how much I could take the overt protection. I mentioned to Danny that he didn't have to do this every time we walked into a room. I think he was unsettled, but then I saw the edges of his mouth curl into a smile. I figured that he'd either back off a little bit or he'd use a more clandestine approach. Either one suited me just fine.

I offered peanut butter sandwiches for lunch—a bit embarrassing compared to the way we'd eaten at Danny's, but I said I'd get to the grocery store and that I could cook when I had some food. He said he didn't care one way or another, but I still had my pride.

We said goodbye to each other, but he made me promise to call if *anything* was suspicious. I watched him disappear down the street.

When I turned to go inside, I noticed a package tucked behind a large plant. I suspiciously picked it up. I started to breathe again when I recognized the return address as my Aunt Thelma's. I took it inside the apartment, bolted the deadbolt, and took a kitchen knife to the edge of the box. I folded back the flaps and looked inside.

The contents included several used books about crystals, clairvoyance, spirit guides, and auras.

No note. I flipped through the books and wondered why Thelma sent them to me. I set everything aside.

After a hot shower, I towel dried my hair and put on a clean pair of jeans and a blue T-shirt. I found another purse, and I had an extra set of keys in my dresser drawer. It took a while to walk to where I had parked my car at the Jeep Tours. The good news was that the car was still there. The bad news was that it had a parking ticket on the windshield.

"Damn it," I said under my breath.

That's when I turned around and saw the blue uniform. I choked down another four-letter word.

Officer J. Hall was two feet away from me.

"Ms. O'Malley," he said.

I'd hoped for at least a day before I had to talk to Sedona's police. I didn't get what I'd wished for.

"I need to ask you some questions about the death of Hugh Rossi. Would you please come with me?"

I grabbed the parking ticket, and in a moment of clarity, I knew who had issued me the citation.

Sedona's detention center is a modern building on the corner of Dry Creek Road. The good news is that the police serve a good cup of coffee. I found myself in a room with Hall and a Sedona detective, and they kept the coffee cup filled, so it was going pretty well. I got edgy after my third cup, but by then I'd told them everything I knew.

They'd shown me pictures of Hugh. Police procedure is to document the scene with photographs. I knew that and cried. Finally, after more tedious questions, I asked, "Am I being charged with anything?" There was an uncomfortable pause before he answered.

"No," the detective finally said, "but don't leave town."

I promised. With that, I set down the coffee and went to find the bathroom to pee. When I came out of the women's restroom, Hall was waiting for me. It occurred to me I might need my Uncle Callaghan's attorney help after all.

"What do you want?" I asked.

"Do you need a ride to your car?"

It would be a hot walk back to my Outback. It would be easier to say that I did need a lift, but I was sick of the questions, and I was tired of Officer Hall.

"No," I answered.

It was a blistering hot walk back to my car. I carried my blazer and wondered why I had worn it. I was exhausted. When I finally got to my car, I had to turn the air conditioning on and waited as a feeble amount of semicool air blasted from the dash vent. I let the air-conditioning run for a while before I could get into my car to drive it. Finally, able to touch the steering wheel, I focused on the next task. I needed to replace my cell phone, so I asked at a service station, when I refilled the gas tank, where the closest cell phone store was located. They gave me directions to a store off Highway 89A on L'Auberge Lane.

I explained the situation to the lady at the cell phone counter, who didn't appear to have any sympathy. I wondered how many times she got the excuse that a customer had lost her cell phone when she plunged over the edge of a cliff?

I had a credit card that I used only for emergency purchases. This was it. I hoped I would have enough money to pay it off before the next month's billing cycle.

I drove to the *Sedona Red Rock News* to find Rebecca. The parking lot was empty except for a black BMW. I tried the door, but it was locked. I pounded on the double-glass doors. A blonde-streaked head popped up over the top of a cubicle to see who was making the racket. It was her.

Rebecca ignored me, so I pounded harder. I could tell she couldn't decide whether or not to let me in. She finally decided to open the door.

"You're alive," she said.

Astute observation is the mark of a true journalist, I thought.

"Not by a whole lot," I answered. "I'll give you an exclusive interview," I offered Rebecca.

Her green eyes shone. "Come in, of course."

We walked to where I'd seen her blonde-streaked head pop up out of the cubicle. Rebecca locked the door behind her.

"Tell me everything," she said as she slid her reporter's pad to her lap.

I gave her the story. When I'd finished, she put her hands to her temples and rubbed them. Her eyes were red.

"I was ready to shoot you," she said. "I cared for Hugh. I really did."

"I'm sorry," I said.

"I've been thinking. I wonder if this has to do with the feature story he was working on?"

Story, I thought. "What story?" I asked.

"Oh, he had some feature article that he thought would make him famous and would launch his career at the *New York Times.* Awards, glory. He lived for that. You know how he was about moving up to the big-league papers."

Yes, I thought.

"He was writing a series of articles for a feature story about the knock-off jewelry sold to tourists as Native American. He'd spent quite a lot of time on it already. He'd interviewed merchants who sold reputable goods, and he was zeroing in on several dealers in town who might be passing off fakes—a fence for the cheap goods."

I looked at my wrist. I slid my turquoise beauty up and down my arm, sure that I couldn't have been taken by such an insidious scheme. That's when I detected a slight black line on my wrist. I figured I must have gotten something under my bracelet. I rubbed the mark with my finger like it was a pencil eraser to paper. It didn't disappear. At this point, Rebecca was intrigued. She walked over closer to my arm and took my hand. She took her reading glasses from the desk and put them on while she put my hand closer to her face. She gasped.

"Don't tell me it's what I think it is," I said. I felt a knot in my stomach when I thought about the amount of money I'd paid for it.

"Take it off," Rebecca insisted.

I took it off my arm and handed it over to her. She examined it closely under the reporter's gaze of the reading glasses. She went over to her desk and opened her desk drawer, where she had a small magnifying glass.

"You keep that in your desk?" I asked.

"Vision is getting bad," she answered. She peered at the bracelet under the magnifying glass.

"What do you think?" I asked, even though I knew the answer.

"I think you need a refund," she said with disgust and handed the bracelet back to me. "Count yourself as another victim of this scam."

"Do you know the name of the merchants Hugh interviewed?" I asked.

"No, but maybe we could get into Hugh's files and find his notes."

We walked back to the cubicle where I'd plied Hugh with my latte and brownies. The empty coffee cup stood on his desk. I felt a catch in my throat.

"I know," Rebecca said to me. "It happens every time I come back here for something. Sometimes, I almost forget what's happened and I catch myself, when I have a question..."

Rebecca stopped talking in midsentence to walk to the computer, and the screen blinked on. She knew the editor's override password. "I'm pretty good at getting what I want," she said. Icons popped up on the screen. Scanning through the file marked "feature articles," Rebecca found his notes. She hit the print button.

"How about a little shopping?" she asked me.

We walked into Ellie Chavez's store. I looked at the certificate of authenticity displayed in the jewelry case. Chavez came out from behind the curtain. I could tell she recognized me.

"Let me guess," I said. "You're surprised."

"Let me explain," she said.

"Okay. Explain. She works for the *Sedona Red Rock News*, so she's going to like to hear this, too."

Ellie claimed she didn't know about the jewelry. She said that she let a friend of her boyfriend work in the shop for weeks at a time while she went to the reservation to take care of her ailing father. It never occurred to her to think that the pieces that she purchased from the reservation artists were being replaced with fakes while she was away. It was only now that some customers had come to her that she had discovered the switch. She told us that she had reported it to the Navajo police and that they were looking for the man who had worked for her. She didn't know how many pieces had been replaced and said that she would refund my money. She'd gone through all the jewelry in the shop to verify that the pieces were authentic.

Since I didn't see anything else I liked, she offered me a choice. Would I be interested in some new pieces she would pick up later? I could come by and exchange the piece I had.

I thought about getting a credit to my Visa, but the lure of a special piece of jewelry brought me back from reason. She showed me pictures of the new line. This jewelry looked to be some of the most detailed Southwestern jewelry I'd ever seen. She offered me 40 percent off due to what had transpired. I reasoned that with Rebecca Fuller poised to write about the jewelry, I would be okay. I left the shop without a refund. I would argue with the bank if I had to. Besides, I wanted to believe her story.

Chapter 11
Sleuthing

IT WAS THE END OF a long day. As I smeared cream on my freshly washed face, I saw in my reflection that the sunburn had faded to a rosy pink. That's when it hit me: To move around Sedona incognito, I could use a disguise. All I needed were some of the props and makeup from the theater, and I could successfully engineer a new identity for myself. Excited at this new prospect, I decided to drive to the theater greenhouse office in the early morning when no one would be around.

Bright and early I walked past the courtyard fountain toward the greenhouse.

I stepped into the office and paused. Something needed to be aired out. I was startled at the ring of my cell phone.

"Hello," I said.

"Ms. O'Malley?" the voice asked on the other end.

"Yes."

"I'm the assistant nurse at Bridgeview where Thelma Parker is a resident. I am calling to inform you that she's been admitted to St. Vincent Hospital. You were listed as a primary contact."

"What's wrong?" I asked, alarmed.

"She's been admitted for an evaluation. Her behavior has become very erratic. I know she's a little on the eccentric side anyway, but all she would talk about is medicine wheels, and we couldn't get her to eat or drink anything. After two days of this, we transported her to St. Vincent. Quite frankly, we were also concerned about dehydration."

She gave me the telephone number for St. Vincent in Portland.

I'd seen my aunt's spirit in the desert. That spirit led me to safety. Had my aunt endangered her well-being to save me?

When I called the nurse on Aunt Thelma's floor, she told me that my aunt was resting and they were giving her IV fluids. When she rang through to the room, Thelma didn't answer. I decided to call again in a little while.

I got to work, in large part to keep my mind off of my aunt's condition, but then the phone rang again.

This time it was Danny.

"Everything okay?" he asked. "You sound upset."

"My aunt isn't well. I called the hospital, but I haven't been able to speak to her."

"Is there anything I can do?"

"No," I said, "but thank you for offering. I have more news. The police already found me, interviewed me, and a detective told me not to leave town."

"So I'll plan to come into town and see you on Monday," he said. "I'll meet you at six o'clock."

"I'll make dinner," I said. "I've got to get back to work now. I'm up to my elbows in it."

I had too much on my mind—the murder, Hugh's death, my sick aunt, Danny's call, and the mounds of paper that were piled on Ryan's desk during his jail detention. I sighed. Whenever I found myself in this kind of disarray, I cleaned. It's a hopeless personality quirk, but I felt like I could move forward if I made some order out of the chaos. And after all, it was part of my job.

I sat down in Ryan's oversized chair and made stacks—unopened mail, opened mail, bills, junk mail, receipts, accounts receivable, accounts payable, letters, and reviews. Once I had the piles sorted, I started on each stack individually. I began with the accounts payable. I would make out the checks and find a way to have Ryan sign them. I could use the public defender, maybe. Or maybe I could ask Officer J. Hall for a favor? He didn't seem to be picking on me like he had before. I had a neat pile of bills in front of me and started writing the checks. I got all the bills paid and filed the notices. Ryan would have an easy account of what went out.

The receipts for the ticket sales were in another pile that I attacked with my organization. It looked like Simon had helped out in my disappearance. He'd placed the bank receipts on the desk with dates and his signature. I looked over the amounts and saw that ticket sales had improved with the community's interest in the murder.

That brought me to my next question: *When will Ryan be released?* I looked at the computer on his desk, now unburied. I still had hours of work ahead of me, but I was making progress. My thinking was beginning to clear.

I tapped the computer to life. I entered *Sedona jail inmates* and got the screen with the box that prompted me to type in a name. The Information Age made knowledge of jail inmates so much easier to gain. Into the box I typed *Ryan O'Malley*, and up popped his status—still in custody, no bail.

The wheels of justice moved slowly, I reminded myself.

I got back to the cleaning at hand. I recycled the junk mail. I clipped the reviews and put them in the file Ryan kept. I added the balances to the accounts receivable. I was almost to the bottom of the pile on the desk when my cell phone rang again. This time it was Rebecca Fuller.

"I need some help," she said.

"Where and when?"

"Meet me in an hour at the newspaper," she answered.

That left me enough time to wipe off the desk and grab the personnel information out of the files. I did both in record time and even dumped out the partially consumed pop cans and leftover Chinese food that was the source of the bad smell I'd encountered when I came into the office. I took some extra costumes and theater makeup along with the information I needed about the actors.

I met up with Rebecca in front of the newspaper. I got into her new BMW. It had cream-colored leather seats.

"Nice car," I said. It had the new-car smell. "Where are we headed? You weren't too specific on the phone."

"We're going to the Sedona Funeral Home."

Not what I expected.

"Hugh only had a stepbrother as next of kin," Rebecca added in explanation, "so we have to make the arrangements. Look, some-one's got to do it."

Chapter 12
Funeral Parlor

THE FUNERAL DIRECTOR IN THE Armani suit didn't know of any bagpipers he could get on short notice in Sedona. He thought he could get a flute player. So it was settled.

Rebecca said she'd take care of the notice in the paper. We planned to release the ashes at the medicine wheel at the Wallow Canyon Trail Vortex, but we agreed we wouldn't tell too many people about the ashes because we didn't want trouble with the National Forest Service.

When we got out of the funeral parlor, I said to Rebecca, "I need a drink." The whole finality of Hugh's death had taken an emotional toll on me.

She looked at her watch. "It's only eleven o'clock. But there's a place down the road. We could get an early lunch."

"I'll have a glass of the house chardonnay," Rebecca said to the waiter and added, "and the watercress salad."

The waiter looked at me for my food order.

"I'll have a gin and tonic," I said.

After the waiter brought me my drink, I said to Rebecca, "After this, I need to buy some new jewelry."

"You don't take death well," Rebecca said.

"No, I don't," I said. "Plus, I've got rehearsal this afternoon. We start practice for *Romeo and Juliet* for the second part of the summer season. I'm not ready. And my brother is still in jail."

When the waiter brought Rebecca the salad, I ordered the same. It was filled with caramelized pecans, shaved apples, and gorgonzola.

"Chavez told me she'd have the new jewelry," I said as I thought about where we could shop. And I was determined to get the exchange on my bracelet.

Rebecca took a bite of her salad. She had this way of eating that made her look good. Most people can't chew and look very attractive, but Rebecca seemed to have it down. When she took a sip of her chardonnay, a little green-eyed jealously sprouted in me. "So what's your crutch? It's human nature to have one. If you know it, at least you recognize it when it rears its head."

Rebecca poked at the shaved apples. "Men and relationships," she said in an unguarded way—like she'd come to terms with her humanness. "I like men who like other women. It's been that way since fifth grade. It started with Michael, who liked Stephanie when I liked him—a love triangle. I did everything I could to get him to like me, but he only had eyes for Stephanie."

"So what happened?" I asked.

"I punched Michael in the nose and got sent home for the day, but it was worth it."

Sexual tension does that to women.

She added, "Stephanie didn't like him after that. She thought he was a crybaby. Steph and I were best friends after that."

We both ordered dessert. It appeared that Rebecca and I might even be able to head down the road toward friendship. The waiter brought warm berry crisps with vanilla ice cream. I figured I was making progress, since I hadn't been able to touch anything with berries in it since I'd come across my copulating husband.

After we paid our check, I sat back down again—fast.

"What is it?" Rebecca asked, surprised.

"Do you see that man in the booth over there?" I tipped my head in the direction I wanted her to look.

She peeked over the top of the imitation-leather booth in the direction I'd bobbled my head. She sat back down. "That's Matthew Bell. He's a high roller in real estate in Sedona."

"He was my brother's date the night Ryan was arrested," I added.

"So are you going to ask him if he killed someone?"

I glared at Rebecca. "It doesn't work like that. Now let's get out of here before the entire restaurant notices us looking at him."

Chapter 13
Jewelry Exchange

At Chavez's store, a hand-printed sign read CLOSED. "What do you make of that?" Rebecca asked. "She said she'd be open with the new jewelry."

"My boyfriend can find out about Chavez," I said. I made a mental note to myself to ask Danny if he knew her.

"Boyfriend?" Rebecca asked with an arched brow. "You didn't tell me that Danny was your boyfriend."

I looked at her like a cat looks at a mouse. "You keep your hands off of him. Just because I like him, doesn't mean you should." I hadn't told her about my relationship with Danny.

"Good point," she agreed.

Since it looked like I wouldn't be able to exchange my bracelet today, I decided I needed coffee if I expected to be able to function into the evening. I had a lot of work ahead of me.

"Coffee?" I suggested.

"Sure," Rebecca answered, "I could use some caffeine about now."

My cell phone interrupted us. Rebecca saw a drive-through coffee kiosk and turned into the parking lot. We were idling behind a Ford pickup. I answered without checking the incoming telephone number first. That was a mistake. I was sorry when I heard the voice.

"It's my husband," I whispered to Rebecca.

That's when he proceeded to yell. He always yelled at me about something. It's a good thing we didn't have any children. He got into a money tirade and then he started to launch into something about a missing tool. I didn't let him finish, because by this time he'd been going on for too long. I changed the subject and said, "Did you sign the divorce papers?"

He didn't answer. I couldn't stand passive-aggressive. That was the other side of Phil. I really don't know why I married him. But in all fairness, he acted like a saint before we got married. He came over and helped me with any kind of project I'd started. He was a different person then. That wasn't the Phil I was married to now. There was only that silence on the other end of the telephone line. I shook my cell phone like I could shake Phil out of the receiver.

"Hello," I said again, "are you there, Phil?"

I wanted to add *asshole* after his name. Rebecca, who had been listening to at least one end of this conversation, caught the drift.

Finally, he spoke. Actually, he yelled. "Look, I don't want any money taken from the account. Do you understand? Next time you'll hear from my attorney."

He hung up. He had to have the last word. I really had no idea what he was talking about. I'd been living off my theater pay. I hadn't touched any money (and, I might add, there wasn't much to touch). The house sale money was held in trust by the trust company. There were only a few hundred dollars in the joint account.

I thought I should call my attorney, but when I thought about his charge of $250 an hour, I decided I'd wait. Phil was a hothead, but I hadn't done anything wrong, so why should I spend money so my attorney could write his attorney to tell Phil the same thing I had just said on the phone?

Rebecca looked at me, a little sorry. She'd ordered a large double-shot latte for both of us. She passed one to me. I took a sip and sighed. "Let's go find a jewelry shop that's open," I said.

"Look," Rebecca said after we'd found a New Age jewelry store, "I know it's only your business, but maybe you could be nicer to Phil to get what you want."

I glared at her. But the thing about her suggestion was that she was right. Phil brought out the worst in me. What I'd realized is that relationships have a beginning and an end. With a marriage you expect the end to come after the "death" part in the wedding vows. But it doesn't always work that way. Ask the percentage of the population who found out that no matter how hard they tried, no matter how they had willed it not to, the relationship failed. When you wake up to an empty bed, you're reminded of it.

Standing in Soul Creations Jewelry, I could feel my heart pound as the endorphins kicked in at the thought of a jewelry purchase. However, just as quickly, my hormones skidded to an abrupt halt; behind me was Officer J. Hall.

What is he doing here, now?

I decided to do my best to ignore him. I had that thought firmly in mind while I looked into the glass case and caught my first glimpse of the most exquisite ring I've ever seen. I gasped at a deep-blue sapphire wrapped in white-gold like waves lapping at the beach shores of St. Thomas. The salesperson with handsome, angular features walked over to me.

"Exquisite, isn't it?" he said. "You have exceptional taste. I just put it out. Do you want to try it on?"

"Oh, yes," I said in a daze.

Rebecca, who'd caught my expression, came to my side. I slipped it onto my finger on my right hand and moved my hand back and forth. Even as a dark-blue stone, the ring caught the light. For the time being, I'd forgotten that J. Hall was in the shop. But I remembered when I saw his reflection in the mirror on the counter. He was behind me—at a discreet distance—but watching.

I turned the little white tag on the band and saw the price. I wiggled the beauty off my finger and gave it back to the clerk. "I'm just looking," I said, disappointed. I needed my refund from Chavez first.

The clerk nodded.

Rebecca and I left the store to shop for perfume—her suggestion, but clearly a poor substitute for jewelry. Hall had disappeared.

"What's with that cop and you?" Rebecca asked as we walked by the courtyard fountain toward the perfume shop. "I thought you had a boyfriend. How long has he had a thing for you?"

That cop and me?

"Men are transparent," Rebecca went on. "I don't think it could be any more obvious. Has he ever talked to you besides to give you a ticket?"

"At the police station," I answered.

Rebecca looked at me with her cat-green eyes. "Tell me."

"There's nothing to tell. It was about Hugh and where I'd been." I added, "And that I shouldn't leave Sedona. That cop kind of stuff."

"Oh," she said as she twisted a lock of her blonde-streaked hair. "I think you need to go out with him."

"I'm a monogamist," I said in protest.

Wow. Still in the legal process of a contentious divorce, my life had clearly morphed—a soon-to-be ex-husband screaming at me, sleeping with Danny, who had saved my life, and now a lustful cop after me. Things were getting complicated.

"Why date Hall?" I asked for some objectivity.

"Keep your options open is all I'm recommending," Rebecca said. "And I think you still have some personal work regarding relationships," she added.

Now that's an understatement. I looked up at a balcony shop, where I could imagine Juliet's head out the window, waiting for Romeo. Juliet could have used a friend like Rebecca. Juliet could have used a girlfriend to say, "Forget Romeo…there are other fish in the sea…" and she could have gone on to better things in her life besides the fate that awaited her.

Chapter 14
Yoga

AFTER THE EARLY REHEARSAL OF *Romeo and Juliet,* which looked to be smooth sailing, I avoided drinks with the cast afterward and begged off with the excuse that I hadn't been to my yoga class for weeks, and that if I wanted to continue to fit into my clothes, I'd need to get there. I'd signed up for drop-in yoga when I'd moved to Sedona. Now, I'm not a yogi, but yoga helped me to find something constructive to center my life around. Yoga was worth exploration, and I'd found its benefits.

And at this point, I'd almost set aside that sense of apprehension that followed me since I'd been back in Sedona. I'd almost let go of that looking-over-my-shoulder-at-every-corner behavior. It takes a kind of energy that can't be sustained, and I knew I had to live my life. And let's face it, I was a little frustrated about Danny, whom I hadn't heard much from. *Have sex with a guy, and then they don't or hardly call. That happens way too much in life.*

I decided to call Thelma. The assisted living center had called that morning, and doctors indicated that she was better—the IV liquids had done the trick—and she had left the hospital. She didn't pick up the phone. I'd try to call her later in the evening.

At the apartment, I gave Karma a chew toy and a bowl of fresh water, put on my yoga clothes—the capri-length black pants with the printed yoga top with the Chinese symbol for long life—and drove to class. I needed a little extra time before class began to listen to the meditation music the teacher played and to ground myself and turn inward before we began the poses. It's like the premeditation before the meditation.

Upon arriving at the community center, I took off my shoes and walked onto the smooth wood floors. The Zen music flowed into my stressed ears, and I knew this was when I needed yoga the most. I rolled out my sticky mat and went to the floor, and I felt my back against the hard wood. I bent my knees and put my hands to my side with palms up. In my premeditative pose, I attempted to let the stress of my estranged husband, the guilt of Hugh's death, the physical relationship with Danny, and all the subliminal feelings about Hall drip through my body and transcend into something higher, something ethereal, something that made sense out of my goddamn existence. Yoga wasn't always enough. But at least it was a start—a fledging attempt at finding something that didn't exist on the earth, something that was greater than me, a spiritual presence that filled me full of white light and Zen.

Somehow, I thought, *if I can find that center, I can help Ryan, I will finish this recklessness with my estranged husband, and I'll be present for Danny or figure out what I'm doing in a relationship with a medicine man.*

During the class time, I went through my poses with the intensity of exploration and adjustments: downward dog, triangle, child pose, and warrior pose as metaphors of my life…and where was I now?

We were in the final stage of yoga—the calming reflective time where we were given permission to relax and go inward—when my instructor came over to me and said that I was thinking too much.

It shows. She covered my eyes with a towel to help me go back into myself. And I tried. But the events in the last weeks were more than I was able to hold back, and the images of the desert and Thelma and Kuruk couldn't find a way out of my consciousness. And the part that bothered me the most was the vision of Officer J. Hall, who wouldn't leave my thoughts no matter how hard I tried to get him out. It was as if he taunted me to release him into the karmic air.

After the *namaste*, I felt a little better.

I stood at my car and fiddled with my keys. It was dark. I had my yoga bag tucked under my arm, my water bottle in one hand, and my keys in the other. I didn't hear any footsteps until I had the driver's side door open and I had one foot inside the car. I remember a horrific shove, and I felt my head crack against the windshield. Blood welled up in my mouth and white diamonds flashed around me.

My legs crumpled to the dark pavement, and I added rubies and sapphires to the orchestra of light. As I went down toward the asphalt, I wondered if this is what it felt like when you're going to die. Then I don't remember much.

Finally, I heard my name float over a celestial boundary. My vision began to clear and what was nebulous came into focus. As I still strained to see clearly, I was finally able to make out the face of Officer J. Hall as he hovered over me.

His blue eyes danced in the community-center lights.

The wail of the ambulance broke through the still night air, and I willed my brain to remember what had happened. The siren grew, and then I heard the slams of vehicle doors and heard the voices of the emergency medical technicians and saw them wheel the gurney toward me. They lifted me into the ambulance and transported me to Sedona's Verde Valley Medical Center.

As luck would have it, a plastic surgeon was on call that evening, and I landed in a hospital room for recovery. The diagnosis was that I'd suffered a concussion, plus I needed about nine stitches on my forehead, and I'd be required to spend the night at the medical center. When the nurse delivered the news, I begged for reconsideration. "Do you know someone's trying to kill me?"

The well-rounded nurse looked at me without an ounce of sympathy. "You have a concussion. If fluid builds in your brain, and no one is around, you will die. I've seen it happen." And with that, she took my empty plastic water bottle and went to get it refilled.

When she came back, she'd softened a little. "Besides, I'm here tonight, and I'll alert the morning shift nurse to keep an eye out. Also, there's someone here to see you, and I know he won't let anything happen to you."

With that, she exited through the doorway. Through the other side of the door came the toned, tanned, and blue-eyed Officer J. Hall. And this time, he wasn't in his uniform. He had on Levi jeans and a J. Crew cotton dress shirt, open at the collar. And when he sat down next to me, I noticed that he smelled good—like citrus—and it helped to replace the smell of hospital disinfectant.

I did everything to squelch the *he's-attractive* intake of air. Fortunately for me, my nurse appeared. She scribbled notes and said, "I'll leave you two alone."

Hall reached over and patted my knee. "Glad to see you're alive," he said as I saw a blush of red on his cheeks.

"What happened?" I asked even though I was in the haze of painkillers and probably wouldn't remember his answer.

"I was going to ask you the same question."

I told him that I thought someone had come up from behind me. I couldn't be sure, though. He had a notebook and wrote down what I said even though I didn't have a whole lot to offer. I was curious about why he'd come to talk to me in his off-duty attire.

"What makes you ask?" he said.

"This is the first time I haven't seen you in uniform."

And if you're off duty, why you? Why not someone else? But thanks to the painkillers, holding two thoughts together seemed impossible, and I pretty much forgot everything.

"I'll come back later," he said.

I wasn't an outstanding conversationalist. Then I remembered something. I needed a favor. I tried to ask before the opiates took over again.

"I need some help—will you let my dog out? And feed her in the morning?"

I didn't know where my purse was, but I reached for something and forgot what I was looking for. I felt a sharp stab of pain through my forehead.

"Need the nurse?" Hall asked.

Before I could answer, she appeared. "Time for some rest," she said.

"Just a few more minutes," Hall asked politely. "I need directions to her house to take care of her dog. She's also looking for her bag."

The nurse went to get it. When she came back, I fished inside for my keys and rattled off my address.

"Is anything missing?" Hall asked.

I pulled out my wallet and everything seemed to be in order. No missing credit cards. No missing money.

"I think everything is here," I answered. *Why didn't they take my purse?*

"What's your dog's name?" Hall asked.

"Karma," I answered.

My cell phone interrupted us.

"Hey," Rebecca said when I answered. "I've been going through Hugh's notes at his apartment, and he was on to something with the jewelry thing."

"How'd you get into his apartment?" I asked.

"He'd given me a key," she said. "A lot of us had one," she added. "If you'd have stuck around longer, you'd have had one too. That's why I told you to stay away from him. I think half of the women in Sedona own a key to Hugh's apartment. Once in a while he'd get the locks changed, so women wouldn't bump into each other—while—oh, you know what I mean."

I had a clear visual in my mind.

"Why don't you meet me here at his apartment? I'll show you what I found."

I wanted to, but Hall and my nurse wouldn't be happy. Besides, Officer J. Hall had agreed to take care of Karma, and I was beginning to think some sleep would be okay.

"I can't," I said. "I'm at the Verde Valley Medical Center. And I'm being held here by a nurse who might call the police if I try to escape."

A low whistle came through the phone. "What happened?"

I explained everything I knew, which wasn't much.

"Are you going to tell your boyfriend?" she asked.

"No," I said. "At least not right now."

"Get some rest. I'll call you tomorrow and tell you everything I find out." And with that, Rebecca disconnected.

Hall set his business card next to my plastic water bottle and told me not to worry about my dog. I planned to call Rebecca back, but my nurse took my cell phone. She said something about hospital protocol and oxygen.

I listened as Hall's and my nurse's voices faded outside of my room.

I woke up to my hospital phone ringing. The clock on the wall read six o'clock in the morning.

It was Thelma's frail voice.

How did she know I'm in the hospital? I remembered that she always knew things like that.

"Did you get the books?" she asked.

"Yes, but…"

Thelma cut me off before I could finish my sentence, uncharacteristic of her.

"I don't have much time left," she said.

"I'm sure you're okay," I said in denial. "I love you," I added.

After we said our goodbyes, I cried.

Chapter 15
Discharge

I TOOK A CAB TO my apartment. I felt some gratitude creep into the deep fissure of my life. *Maybe Hall isn't such a jerk. After all, he took care of my dog.* I took that attitude inside and found Karma asleep on the couch with Hall. She looked content and barely lifted her head to acknowledge me.

"Sleep around, Karma, and see what you get," I said in a whisper.

I went to make coffee. I scooped up my best French roast beans and whirled them until they were the perfect consistency. I did this because I needed time to figure out how I felt about Hall. Rebecca's advice rambled through my brain.

I thought my time in the kitchen would be a discreet way for Hall to get up and get ready to go. But after I watched the first chug of water pump through the coffee pot, I went out and found Hall and Karma in about the same position as before. Neither one seemed to be moving fast, and both looked too comfortable.

I poured kibble in Karma's stainless steel bowl, and that brought success, at least with Karma, when she reluctantly removed herself from her nest next to Hall.

"Sleep around," I said to Karma. She looked at me with her sable-brown eyes.

Give her a round of fetch, and she'd follow a guy anywhere.

I was in the middle of this thought when Hall walked into the kitchen. "I planned to feed her," he said.

I handed him a coffee mug. "Creamer is in the refrigerator and sugar is in the cupboard," I said. "And then it's time for you to go."

Karma whined. The final straw was when Hall went in for a kiss. I exploded. "Out," I said, much louder than I expected.

He tried to say something, but I pointed at the door.

I sat down on the couch where it was still warm from where Karma and Hall had spent the night. Karma came over and nuzzled my hand. I gave her long strokes over her head.

"Stay away from cops," I whispered to her as I scratched her behind the ears.

I went to get a coffee refill and spotted Thelma's books. She'd mentioned them in our last conversation. *How can these books help me?* I remembered she liked to write in them because it helped her form her ideas. As I skimmed through the pages of my aunt's books, something caught my eye. It read: *Psychometry, Greek, from psyche meaning soul, and metron meaning to measure,* in Thelma's perfect cursive. She'd also written that it was a sensation like vibration or coldness she received from the energy of an object that assisted her with her clairvoyance.

I'd felt the vibration at the vortex, and I knew that Thelma was able to sense vibrations from objects. It's also how the O'Malley family had found water for generations. I saw that she'd made a notation about jewelry as a good transmitter of energy by an owner. Setting the books down, my guilt revisited me as I thought about the lost opportunities to learn from her. I saw my teenage years with my aunt, and the memories were so clear that I had to sit down. It was like a movie playing in my mind. I'd never had this kind of vision before. *Why now? Why do I see a miniature movie clip of my life?*

I decided to wear my hair up since I couldn't wash it very well with my stitches. I took a couple Advil and put on a pair of jeans—the skinny-legged ones—along with my black, midlength boots and a new white T-shirt that made my breasts look good. I put on the turquoise jewelry—a large necklace and earrings—that my Aunt Thelma had given me.

I had the O'Malley power. Wasn't it time to use it? It was too early in the morning for my attorney to answer, but I left a message anyway. I needed to speak to him right away. I patted Karma on the head and gave her a treat. "Guard the apartment," I said to her.

I needed to talk to my brother. I drove to the Sedona Detention Center at the intersection of Highway 89A and Dry Creek Road. I followed the signs to visit detainees. I segued to the counter and completed a form with a stubble pencil. An arrow pointed to where I had to present my identification.

A cop told me to sit until I heard my name. I waited for about thirty minutes. Finally, the cop escorted me through a metal detector to a cubicle with a telephone receiver and a plastic chair. There was a large window of Plexiglas between me and where I expected my brother to appear. The cop left. I sat and waited. Ryan appeared in a prison-issue jumpsuit. He was haggard-looking with blue-black stubble on his face.

I picked up the receiver. He picked up his on the other side of the Plexiglas.

"Glad to see you."

"Holding up okay?" I asked.

"Not so good."

The air sat stagnant between us.

"It's bad," he said. "Please keep the theater going until I can get released," he pleaded. "I didn't kill Nicole. You've got to believe that."

"I know."

I didn't ask him about the drugs. My hands sweated.

"A public defender came to see me today," he said as he got up to leave. His shoulders dropped as he walked back with a cop toward his cell.

I worked on some sets until I heard the door open and Louise walked in. Louise was stunning, and the box office receipts continued to sold-out crowds—reviving the financial part of the theater even more.

"Congratulations," I said to Louise when she arrived. "The audience loves you."

She blushed. "I'm happy about that."

"Sit down," I invited her, "so we can talk about the next play." I sewed on a costume and asked, "Did you know Nicole before this summer?"

"What do you mean?" Louise asked.

"I wondered about your experience—what other plays you've understudied? So we can make a decision about auditions." I handed Louise the blue silk and chemise dress that she wore from the balcony when she called for Romeo. "Try this on. We'll talk later. But I'd like to know if you knew Nicole before this summer."

"I worked with Nicole for a short time last summer."

She left it off her résumé.

"Was that at the theater in Ashland?"

"Yes. It was at the Shakespearean theater there. And it was difficult in every sense of the word—not the acting, of course. I'm fully up for that—but Nicole, her diva-ship, made things miserable for everyone."

"There must be a reason why you didn't mention it to Ryan or to me."

She looked uncomfortable. "You remember the director there, John Bauer?"

Oh, I remember him, I thought. *He's a skirt chaser. He put the moves on me.*

"Well, I wanted that part. And I know what you're thinking because I'd heard the rumors about him. But I thought I could handle it. I didn't think I'd be his next conquest, and I thought I could convince him I should be the lead."

"But it didn't turn out that way?"

Louise looked embarrassed. "He took me out, he promised me the world, he got me in bed, and he didn't give me the part. I left in the middle of the season. He said if anyone called for a reference, he'd tell them I was awful—on stage and in bed."

"Before that happened, would you take Nicole's place often?"

"Listen, I didn't kill Nicole. Yes, I figured I'd end up with this job in Sedona, but I thought it would be because she'd be fired for her erratic performances—not murdered. And I didn't have to worry about Ryan attempting to get me between the sheets and all, given that the whole theater community knows he's gay."

She took the costume out of my hands and went back into her dressing room.

I felt a current of air, and in walked Simon. "I thought I heard Louise," he said as he looked around.

"She went to her dressing room. I might as well ask you now—where were you when Nicole was murdered?"

"You think I killed Nicole?" Simon blurted out, looking hurt.

"Well, you and Nicole were at each other," I reminded him.

"I didn't kill her. Nicole bullied me, and I resented her for that. She made me feel like I was in high school again, but I didn't kill her. I couldn't hurt anyone." Simon softened his face. "Since you're asking, I'll tell you about a rumor I heard. Your brother was being blackmailed," he said.

"Who's doing it?" I asked, "And what about?"

"I don't know the particulars," he answered, "but you should ask Kayla. She knows a lot of what goes on around the theater—things that no one likes to talk about." Simon lifted his big frame out of the chair. "I'm going to read over some of the new scripts," he said. "Let me know when we're ready to start."

Jake Jordan came in after Simon had left. He was wearing bike shorts and his helmet.

"How's the bike?" I asked.

"I'm attempting to leave a small carbon footprint in the world," he answered.

"Been on any hikes lately?"

"To the Airport Vortex," he answered. "It's the only one I hadn't been to yet."

He took off his helmet and sweat streaked down his face. I looked at his T-shirt. On the front was a native flute player.

"Nice shirt," I said.

"They're hot right now," he said. "It's a new company in West Sedona. They take the red rock and mix it with some other stuff that dyes the shirts this color. The company is growing. As a matter of fact, I've been offered a job there. Of course, I hope to keep my acting job, too."

I've got to ask him, I thought.

"So, how were you and Nicole getting along—before she was killed?"

Jake laughed. "You're not good at this. But since you're my boss's sister, I'll answer the question."

Jake went on to explain that his health-minded approach and Nicole's party drug ways were at odds with each other. But that was it as far as any kind of conflict. He took out his script and went back to his dressing room to start memorizing his lines.

Megan Kennedy came through the greenhouse office door. She was the most talented of all the cast. I knew from her résumé that she had a Master's Degree in chemistry.

"How's everything?" I asked her after she refilled her water bottle from the cooler in the office.

"Cool," she said.

"Here's the script we want you to look over," I said. "Are you planning to work in the theater this fall?"

"I'm saving for a trip to Africa," she said, "but I don't have enough money yet. So I plan to work for a few more months before I take off."

"Do you know who might have killed Nicole?"

"No," she answered.

"Know anything about it?"

"No."

"Angry?" I asked.

"No," she answered.

And with that, she took her script and departed.

When Kayla Canup came by for her costume fitting later in the day, I asked if she could stop by my apartment about four o'clock for a glass of wine. Kayla and I got along pretty well and would occasionally have wine together in the afternoon by the pool. She was related to Ryan and me as some kind of shirttail cousin, although we decided, since we both worked the theater circuit, we wouldn't make it public knowledge. We didn't really know each other until we were older, so we didn't have all sorts of common childhood memories. But we did know we were connected in a bond as family.

She agreed to meet me at four o'clock.

Simon had left and come back in the stage door as I was ready to leave for the day. I'd almost finished.

"What's up?" I asked Simon as he came over to where I was painting a set. Danny was coming to dinner—an event I looked forward to. He'd given me a call to confirm.

"My payroll check bounced," he announced with irritation. "I tried to cash it a half hour ago."

But the ledger showed healthy accounts.

"I can't work for free, Lizzy."

I assured him it must be some kind of mistake. I promised to look into it, and I wrote him a check from my bank account. Not that I had much, but I had enough to cover his wages. I wasn't sure what I'd do if the other actors' checks bounced.

Chapter 16

A Clue

WHILE I WAS BOILING WATER for the pasta, I heard a knock on my door. It was Kayla. I invited her inside and poured her a tall glass of Chianti.

"Yum," she said, "dinner smells good." We sat at my kitchen table, which was set with a mishmash of tableware that I'd brought to Sedona. I also had a small bouquet of flowers in the center.

"Who's the special someone?"

I told her about Danny.

"I'm jealous," she said.

I felt guilty I hadn't invited her for dinner, but I'd hoped for some time alone with Danny.

"No way!" she answered as if she'd read my mind. "Don't even think about it. Three's a crowd."

Kayla had her own gift of intuition.

I'd been sitting on the question for so long. "Do you know something about the theater and blackmail?" I asked.

"It's only speculation," she answered.

"Okay," I said, "what's the gossip?" I got up and took the magnetic pad off the refrigerator. "I'll take notes."

"I heard this at the Oak Creek Brewery. The bartender is my boyfriend. And by the way, he makes a fabulous martini."

I wrote down *bartender, Oak Creek Brewery and Grill*. I added a quick sketch of a martini glass with an olive.

Kayla looked at the drawing. "That's pretty good," she said. (Aunt Thelma told me I'd been an artist in a past life.)

"What about the blackmail?" I asked.

"I overheard two men at the bar talking about a development in West Sedona—the one that Matthew Bell is bankrolling. One of them said that Matthew Bell wouldn't be able to afford much of anything anymore."

Matthew Bell was Ryan's date. *Did Ryan finance Matthew instead of the other way around?* I thought. *And what does this mean for the future of the theater?* There was speculation that a development would include a theater as an anchor business with housing, entertainment, and businesses in one community.

I asked Kayla if she recognized either of the men at the bar.

"No." But she added, "My boyfriend said he called a cab for them because they were too drunk to drive. The driver had to take them all the way to Cottonwood. I guess the cabbie threatened to call the police to make them cough up the money if they didn't pay the fare in advance. These guys looked like they'd stiff the driver for it."

"Do you know them by the description?" she asked me.

I wrote down *Cottonwood, sleazeballs, Nicole's apartment*.

"I might," I said. I was about to explain it to her when I heard the television news with a breaking report: A fire threatened several homes in an exclusive, gated community in West Sedona. Live footage showed flames licking at the remaining structure while firefighters aimed hoses at it.

Kayla turned to watch, and I heard her quick intake of air.

"That's Matthew Bell's house," she gasped.

Before I could respond, I heard a knock at my front door. I looked out my peep-hole and saw that it was Danny. I undid the dead bolt and the lock and went for a hug. We stayed like that for a while before Kayla, who'd come into the living room to see what was going on, cleared her throat.

"Kayla, this is Danny. Danny, this is Kayla."

"I was just on my way out. Thanks for the wine, Lizzy."

I said she didn't have to leave right away, but she said she was meeting her boyfriend tonight after his shift. When she passed her wine glass to me, I saw Kayla's future in a flash like a Charlie Chaplin movie.

"Kayla," I said, "He's more than a passing boyfriend."

She looked at me, surprised. "Funny you should say that," she said, "because I had the feeling he might be the one."

"I think you should explore the relationship at a deeper level," I added.

I didn't tell her about the four kids and the picket fence with the trailing roses climbing on it and the giant tomatoes in the backyard. I decided she could figure it out.

"Hey, Kayla," I said, "you okay with switching cars with me for a little while? Sedona police are a thorn in my side. I'd like to be able to move around a little more freely." I added, "Just be careful."

Kayla paused and shrugged. That was the thing I liked about Kayla.

And with that, she handed me the keys to her Jeep, and I gave her the keys to my Outback. "The tank is full."

Kayla waved as she left.

I refilled my wine and handed Danny a full glass. I checked on the pasta sauce simmering on the back of the stove and put a little more of the red wine in it. I stirred and took a taste.

I drained the pasta noodles and rinsed them in the sink. I opened the refrigerator and took out the salad and lightly tossed it in some olive oil, balsamic vinegar, salt, and pepper.

Danny and I went into the living room for some predinner conversation, but that didn't last long because after a few sips of Chianti we were kissing.

My cell phone interrupted us.

I wasn't going to answer, but I reconsidered when I thought it might be Rebecca. I had not heard from her since I was in the hospital.

Actually, it was Kayla, who said she hoped she wasn't interrupting anything.

I told her that she wasn't, and she said she was sorry to hear that, but she wanted to let me know that her bartender boyfriend had asked her to marry him and she'd accepted. Was there anything else she needed to know from me?

I hesitated. What were these newfound visions that flowed? Was it the future?

I told Kayla she had to listen to her heart, and if her heart told her yes, then she'd done the right thing.

A nagging concern about Rebecca was growing into a full-scale worry.

This ability to see something in the future was exhilarating and frightening.

Add that to the adrenaline rush people get in the first stages of a full-fledged relationship, and Danny and I were there. We couldn't keep our hands off each other. Of course, we were still getting to know each other.

But everything seemed to be moving along in a positive way. I knew I shouldn't be involved with someone so soon while a divorce loomed over me, but in the frailty of human beings, I'd succumbed. And I knew if my husband got wind of it, he would use it against me—even though Oregon was a no-fault divorce state and he'd been entwined with a woman in my Egyptian cotton sheets.

After dinner—pasta was perfect, company was even better—we were involved in a chocolate molten cake in individual ramekins (center was a ganache scoop) with a rich Italian decaf roast coffee. We decided to watch a little news to see if we could update ourselves on the whole Matthew Bell house event.

Something was digging at me.

A blonde television reporter with breast implants reported from the scene with fire trucks in the background.

Where is Rebecca? I still hadn't heard from her, even though I'd called and left messages on her voice mail. That question nagged at me.

Chapter 17
More Sleuthing

THE NEXT MORNING, I DECIDED to drop by Hugh's apartment. While I searched for a clean pair of jeans and towel dried my hair, I tripped over the makeup and props I'd brought home from the theater. Danny had left. I'd felt his warm breath on my check as he leaned over to give me a goodbye kiss. I took the blonde wig from the box and adjusted it on top of my head. I went into the bathroom and applied a heavy foundation and blush on the apples of my cheeks. My skin tones were not favorable for a blonde look, but it did advance a drastic change in my appearance.

Karma came into the bathroom to look and sniffed at me.

"What do you think?" I asked her. I thought I looked a little bit like Marilyn Monroe when I went for the blue eyeliner and a heavy dose of mascara. I finished with a brighter-than-normal shade of red lipstick. Voila! I had undergone a metamorphosis. And that was exactly what I'd planned.

No one was scheduled to be at the theater until four o'clock.

I rolled into Hugh's apartment's lot and parked in an unobtrusive place in the back where the cottonwoods hung low. It pretty much made the car disappear—at least it didn't look too obvious. I'd also mixed some red-rock dust with a little of my bottled water and swished it across Kayla's license plate.

Karma had shade, and it wasn't too hot yet, with a slight breeze in the early morning. I poured some of my water from my bottle into one of those collapsible dog bowls. I'd figured I'd have to get a little rough with the apartment lock, so I brought my theater tools and pulled on some latex gloves. I snapped them on and cracked the windows for Karma. I'd need to get in and out of the apartment—fast.

Since Hugh didn't have a nearby next of kin, I didn't know who would be cleaning out his place or if I might bump into somebody.

And that's when Danny called, and we had our first fight. Now, the first fight has to happen. It could be after the first slight or the first misstep or the first thing that someone does that reminds someone of his or her ex. The question is, how will a couple maneuver around it?

I think he called to check in with me. I felt like he was smothering me. We'd only been away from each other for a couple of hours. Yes, I should have accepted that he cared about me, but what I heard is that he didn't appreciate my independence and that he wanted to be closer to me than I was ready to accept. And that can be a defining moment in any relationship. So I shot back to leave me alone. And most men don't understand the nuances of that kind of comment.

And, most often, those kinds of remarks are not met with the best of responses.

Danny's silence sat on the other end of the line. He didn't know me well enough to say the words to assuage my insecurity, my guilt, and my anguish from failures in my life.

And with that, I hung up. It wasn't easy being involved with me.

So I pacified myself as I got back to the task at hand. I tried the credit card on the apartment door lock, but it only opened a fraction of what I'd hoped. I took a large wrench out of my bag of tricks, looked around to make sure no one was watching, and pummeled the lock. It gave way to sheer force. It was a pity that I'd had to hack my way into the apartment, since half of the female population in Sedona owned a key. It was a feeble attempt at reconciliation toward the ache in my heart.

Inside Hugh's apartment, an overstuffed caramel-colored leather couch sat along one wall and a black leather recliner faced a large flat-screen television. A functional dining room table seated four. The kitchen held a food processor, pro-chef knives, and top-of-the-line cookware. I ran my hand over the other objects on his counter. I got a slight vibration over the coffeemaker, but no visions.

I passed down a hallway toward his office.

Inside his office, I surveyed his bookshelf. He had books about the Navajo and other tribes, past lives, channeling, soul fights, chakras, aura readings, medicine cards, power animals, and the energy fields of Sedona. Hugh was a little more metaphysical than I'd thought. I sat down in Hugh's leather chair and tried to clear my mind in a meditative-like trance. I cleared my auras, I cleared my chakras, and I tried to clear the guilt-ridden junk out of my head. I felt a small pulsation, but it stopped right away. I went back to a meditative pose.

If only my aunt could see me now.

That's when I saw a key lock under the left side of the desk. I rummaged around the inside of the desk to find a key. Nothing. I took a heavy paper clip and worked it in the desk drawer lock like in the movies. I decided to use the same method I'd used on the front door. Granted, there had to be a key, and apparently Rebecca had found it. But I wasn't Rebecca, and Karma was getting hot in the car, so I smashed the lock. It felt good. I found a folder, took it out of the drawer, and spread out the contents on the desk. It was a working file that included a map of a section of the Navajo Nation. An aerial radiation survey showed flight areas and dozens of abandoned uranium mines. There were at least nine in the Cameron-Tuba City area and about the same number in the Bidahochi location. More were marked in the Monument Valley, Four Corners, and Chinle.

I sat back in Hugh's chair and contemplated the findings. The Navajo Nation was a Swiss cheese of abandoned mines. And of particular interest to me was the Cameron-Tuba City area that was North of Flagstaff and, consequently, not that far from Sedona because Hugh had red X's over two of them. I put the entire file with the map into my bag. I was sure I was retracing Rebecca's steps. I had my pack and my cell phone. *What can go wrong?*

Chapter 18

The Mine

ABANDONED MINES SCATTERED ACROSS THE Navajo Reservation had created health-related concerns about the radiation still being emitted from them. The map in Hugh's file showed the level of radiation contamination via samples collected from aerial photography.

But something had led Hugh to draw X's over these spots.

As I drove to where the map was marked, I realized that there wasn't much in the way of human life between Flagstaff and where I pulled the car over in the middle of nowhere off the highway. I clipped on Karma's leash and grabbed my day pack out of the back. We went in search of an entrance to one of the mines.

After a half hour of searching, Karma began to pull on the leash. I pulled her back. She obeyed for a while and then pulled again. At this point I had her sit and unclipped her leash. She sat and wagged her tag like an umpire brushes off the first-base plate.

"Okay, girl," I said, "show me."

Karma ran off. She sniffed and circled and ran back to me.

I looked for any kind of landmark to orient my position. Karma sprang off again, but when I looked up, she'd disappeared over a low rise.

"Karma, here!" I called.

No dog. I repeated the command.

A Lab head appeared over the rise.

"What is it?" I asked.

She disappeared again. When I got to the top of the rise, I saw a deep laceration in the earth. Karma stood over the top of the hole and peered down into what looked like a black cave entrance. She cocked her head and stared at me with her brown eyes.

I thought I heard Rebecca's voice. It was faint, but then I wasn't sure if I'd heard anything at all. Karma barked. *What am I going to do about it?* The light didn't penetrate the pit beyond several feet. I took my flashlight out of my backpack and pointed it into the black. The light didn't illuminate more than a few feet. I took a rock, dropped it into the fissure, and waited for a faint sound of rock meeting bottom.

I never heard it. *That's a long way down.*

Karma barked again.

"Rebecca," I hollered. "How did you get in that godforsaken hole?"

No response.

I pulled my cell phone out of my daypack. No signal.

"Shit," I said. "Don't worry. I'm going to save you," I added.

I took out a penlight flashlight, put it between my teeth, and clenched down tight. It wasn't too far from where my jaw was already set.

"I'm coming," I mumbled through the aluminum flashlight casing.

Karma bit into my sweatshirt hood and tried to pull me back as I set my shoes on the first rung of the wooden ladder to descend into the opening. I pushed down the icky feeling in my throat. Heights for me could bring on full-fledged panic attacks.

Don't look down, I thought. *Push down the fear.*

I'd taken about ten steps on the ladder when I heard the splinter of wood and the sharp crack of the step give way. I was in a free fall toward the bottom.

I finally stopped falling when the rope I'd tied to the top of the ladder held. I swung in an arc back and forth as I considered the common sense that had led me to secure a line to my ankle before I'd started my decent.

Karma barked at the top of the entrance.

Still with the penlight gripped in my teeth, I pointed toward the bottom, but it wasn't strong enough to penetrate the inky black.

Karma's barking turned to an urgent whine. "It's okay," I mumbled through my clenched jaw. I swung in an arc and grabbed what remained of the wooden ladder, but my stomach churned and my heart fell, because no ladder existed anymore—only side braces remained. The blood pounded inside my head from being upside down. I knew that I needed a plan. *Think.*

I tried to pull myself by my hands using the rope. That clearly became futile because the rope was of a width that it prevented me from falling, but not enough to climb. That didn't leave me much of a choice. Turning, I grabbed the daypack and unclipped my pocket knife. I had no idea where bottom was.

Rebecca called again for help. It gave me some orientation. I stopped to check on any kind of premonition: I needed to use every sense I had to survive—even a sixth one. I was about halfway through cutting the rope—cursing under my breath that I had such a dull knife—when an explosion rocked the inside of the shaft from somewhere deep inside the mine.

Rocks rained from above, and my light fell from my clenched jaw.

Karma's whine turned into a frantic bark. She popped her head over the top, desperate to reach me.

"Karma, stay," I commanded.

I needed to take a leap of faith. I'd heard the flashlight hit the bottom, and it didn't sound like it was beyond what I could survive in a fall. With a quick thrust, I severed the remainder of the strands of rope and felt myself free fall to the bottom of the mine shaft.

Thud. My shoulder and back made contact with the bottom of the pit. The wind was knocked out of me, but other than that, no damage. I had only fallen several feet to meet the bottom of the mine pit. It had turned into a fortunate turn of events—if the rope had been much longer, nothing would have broken my fall from the ladder to the ground. I suppressed a chill.

I pulled myself up on my elbow.

My day pack still connected to me, I felt for my larger, more powerful flashlight. Turning it on, I saw that the shaft connected to a tunnel toward the right with low-hanging rocks.

I called out, "Rebecca!"

No answer.

"Rebecca!" I yelled again.

I hurried along the tunnel shaft until I got to the point where it branched in two directions. I needed to open up to my premonitions and my senses. In other words, I needed to use everything I could to get out of this.

Otherwise, I thought, *I might as well flip a coin.*

I took the right tunnel but felt nothing. I was stopped by a wall of rocks. Not sure why I'd come down this way, I was ready to turn back and try the left-handed tunnel. After ten steps of backtracking, I turned back toward the wall of rock.

There's something here, I thought.

I strained to hear or to feel something.

In front of me was a wall of earth and rocks, but it looked different than the other debris in the other tunnel. I started to dig. *This might be totally futile. What am I thinking? Why do I go full-steam into something, just to get myself into trouble? What fatal flaw fractures my personality?*

In the midst of my misery, I heard a cry for help.

"Rebecca!" I yelled.

I dug in the dirt as sweat dripped down my spine. *Does she have air to breathe?* I kept digging. *Push panic away.* A section collapsed and refilled part of what I'd removed, but I kept at it. Finally, I was able to move enough of the debris to move through the rock barrier and come out on the other side. I made my way forward and watched for low-hanging rocks that protruded from the rock ceiling. I was so concerned about looking up that I almost made a fatal error.

That's when a premonition hit me like when I'd flipped through Aunt Thelma's books and saw miniature movie clips. I visualized I was falling, so I pointed my light *down* in front of me. Ahead was a gaping abyss, and there wasn't enough of a path to skirt around the edges. I had no alternative but to jump.

Breathe, I told myself. *You have to do this*, I willed myself. *Will I make it?* I ran full-on and jumped—over the top of the hole and landed with a solid two-legged plant on the other side.

I ran toward Rebecca's cries.

"You look awful as a blonde," Rebecca groaned.

I'd forgotten about my disguise. "You're not fooled?" I quipped.

She sipped from my water bottle. I made a pillow for her head with my sweatshirt. Dried blood crusted in her hair from a gash on the back of her head. Pointing my flashlight at the wound, I used my first aid kit to clean it and apply a bandage. I'd already cut through the ropes that tied her hands behind her.

"How bad is it?" she asked.

"Not too bad, but we've got to figure a way out of here. Can you tell me what happened?"

Rebecca explained that she'd found information in Hugh's apartment and followed the map like I had done. She also told me how she'd been forced into the mine and her hands tied behind her back when she'd found the other entrance.

"We came from that direction," she said pointing the opposite way.

"So there's another way?"

"Yes."

"Who forced you here?" I asked.

"That Chavez woman. And she was with someone else that I couldn't see. They forced me down here and tied my hands."

I pointed the beam of the flashlight around the cavern. It was equipped with tables, chairs, cartons, food, and other supplies. "She'd come around once in a while to check on me and give me some water. Enough to keep me alive."

I didn't want to think about what they were going to do with her over the long haul.

"Any idea what caused the blast?" I asked.

"Dynamite probably. These mines have sticks left in them."

I took the screwdriver feature out of my knife and pried open one of the wooden crates. Pulling out the packing, I discovered hundreds of ready-to-sell faux jewelry items. So this was the center for fenced goods and the heart of the operation. I found turquoise necklaces, rings, and earrings. I put a good-looking pair of earrings in my pocket.

"I think we better get out of here."

That's when I caught a flash of something that didn't look like jewelry. I pointed toward it and gasped.

"What is it?" Rebecca asked as she limped over to me.

I was frozen in time. I didn't want to believe it. I bent over and picked up a smiling Cleveland Indians key chain from the dust. I wiped it off with my shirt and held it up to the light.

"What's with the baseball trinket..." she asked and stopped in midsentence.

"I know the other kidnapper," I said. I'd let someone into my life, and he'd kickbox-punched my heart.

I wasn't going to hurt for long.

We made our way out of the mine the way Rebecca had come with Chavez. It was slow, but it didn't present any of the obstacles that I'd encountered on my way down. I could finally see light shining in. We were close to the entrance when I saw a small stack of dynamite.

"Can you make it the rest of the way by yourself?" I asked.

"You're not thinking what..." she stopped in midsentence. "I don't think that's a good idea. Let's get out of here."

Pragmatic. But not going to happen.

"Time for *you* to get out of here," I said.

It must have been the cadence in my voice or the look on my face, but Rebecca knew that nothing would change the outcome of what was about to happen.

She walked toward the daylight, and I walked toward the dynamite.

I didn't want to blow myself up. I hovered over the stack and reflected on what was happening. Men don't understand what happens to a woman when she opens up in trust and finds she's been betrayed.

I looked in my pack for matches. The fuses were short. *One stick at a time.* By the time I'd made contact with the last one, the first one was almost to the end of the fuse.

I ran.

The explosion rocked the ground underneath me, and I fell to the earth. The sound vibrated through the air with a series of *kaboom, kaboom, kaboom.* And then it was quiet. I remember Rebecca's hand on my back. Her lips moved, and I thought she said my name, but all I heard was the ring of the dynamite as it exploded over and over again in my head. I got the gist by reading her lips. "We need to go," she mouthed as she grabbed me. Still woozy from the blast, I looked toward where the dynamite had detonated. There was no longer an entrance to the mine there.

"Hear that?" Rebecca said. Mostly I heard an incessant ringing in my ears.

"What?" I said.

"It sounds like a dog barking. What would a dog be doing out here in the desert?" she asked.

Chapter 19

The Psychic

I OPENED THE *SEDONA RED ROCK NEWS* the next morning and read the first paragraph of a front-page article by Rebecca Fuller:

Sedona—Sedona police arrested Ellie Chavez, 24 years old, yesterday, in the most recent bust of a counterfeit jewelry ring. Chavez is being held without bail in the Sedona Justice Center for questioning. Consumer loss from the counterfeit ring is estimated to be hundreds of thousands of dollars. Police are searching for an alleged accomplice.

In hindsight, Rebecca and I had been fortunate to find our way back after the explosion thanks to Karma's barking—she remained, as loyal as ever, at the top of the original mine shaft. When we'd gotten back to Sedona, we went to the police and told them everything. The same detective who'd interviewed me about Hugh listened to our story. I gave him the earrings that I'd taken as evidence. Later we found out that Chavez had been on Sedona Police radar for some time.

It was bittersweet that Danny hadn't been caught. If I'd gotten to him first, it wouldn't have gone well for him. I realized the boyfriend that Chavez had referred to when Rebecca and I had gone to her store was Danny. The irony was that it was under my nose the entire time, and I didn't catch it.

Amidst all this, my clairvoyant abilities were evolving in other areas. More and more I'd sense a vibration from an object I touched or passed. If I could learn the nuances, I'd be able to use my sixth-sense gift more fully.

I flipped the newspaper pages toward the horoscope. Aunt Thelma liked to read these daily, and I'd caught the habit. I turned to my sign and read that I'd have some continued challenges in my relationships ahead.

Yeah, I thought. *Tell me about it.*

I stopped on US 89 to buy some rhodochrosite where I'd purchased my Area 51 coffee mug. The spiritual property of rhodochrosite is to heal people emotionally—especially those who feel unloved. The stone makes the wearer face the truth and opens the heart to love. It allows the wearer to cope with painful feelings without denial or resistance.

Rebecca and I had finalized the details of Hugh's memorial and the scattering of his ashes. We planned to say some words for Nicole. It wasn't right to say goodbye to one without the other. Everything should have been in balance, but I was anxious. When I met up with Rebecca, I said, "I've got this feeling that something bad is going to happen."

But neither one of us had the luxury to ponder that for long because of the memorial. The newspaper planned to close for the afternoon service. The first part was to be held at the funeral home with the traditional words and anecdotes. After that, Rebecca and I and a handful of people close to Hugh planned to drive to the trailhead and hike into the vortex. A few laws were going to get stretched when we constructed a medicine wheel and sprinkled Hugh's ashes.

I'd put in a call to my Aunt Thelma, and it was one of the days she didn't remember me. She'd gone to that place in her mind where the dementia and Alzheimer's takes a patient. I'd wanted to talk to her about this rising anxiety and see if she could give me a "reading" about these events, but there was no way to pull her from the tentacles of the disease. *Tomorrow,* I thought hopefully, *she might be lucid.*

The problem was that I had trusted Danny and look where it got me. *Who can I trust?*

It was a funny place to look for it, but I felt a pull in the direction I was headed. I pulled out the business card that I'd been given when I'd bought the Area 51 coffee mug. There was a woman there I wanted to meet named Peace Jones. Inside the novelty store, a woman in her fifties was standing at the counter reading a book.

"Portland girl," she said as I walked in the door.

"I need some help," I answered. "You must be the psychic I've heard about?"

"I knew we'd meet," she laughed.

We introduced ourselves. "By the way," I asked, "How did you get the name Peace?"

"Parents," she said, "don't always do their kids any favors when they give them a name. Mine were all into peace, harmony, and love."

"Oh, no," I said, "don't tell me you have sisters named Harmony and Love?"

"Smart kid."

"That must have been hard in school."

"Tell me about it. Parents joined a commune. I went to college. I studied psychology, philosophy, and dabbled in religion. But nothing seemed to answer my questions. Except," she added, "when I ate the fruit bowl at the Renaissance Fair at Reed College in Portland after I burned my thesis paper."

The Renaissance Fair was the last week of school, late in May, when the seniors burned their thesis papers after they'd gotten their grade. It included days of closure of the private-school campus to anyone except students. The stories of naked slip-and-slides and pharmaceuticals were known to students at other campuses who didn't celebrate with the same kind of notoriety.

"What about the fruit bowl?" I asked.

"The fruit bowl," she said with a laugh, "I almost forgot what I was talking about. I might have just had a flashback."

She came out from behind the counter.

"The fruit bowl was laced with LSD. It was on the last day of the Ren Fair, after I'd eaten of the fruit bowl, that I saw my first UFO."

The whole UFO thing was a little out there—even for me.

"So what did you see?"

"Well, I think I was still on the campus. That was pretty good acid in those days. Things hadn't gotten so bad with drugs—we lived in a different time—when it was all about using drugs to expand one's mind to greater understanding. Kind of like a religion or something. So I'd looked for answers through the hall of academia and found the answer from the fruit bowl and the sky."

She took out some photographs. "This was at the Cow Pie Vortex," she said as she held up a picture. "I was there with a group one evening for a UFO-hunting tour. We'd only just set up the stuff for the talk, and I had my camera out when I saw this object in the sky. I hurried and took this photograph."

I looked more closely at the orb that was suspended in the sky. It didn't look like anything from this world.

"When I got back, I printed this. I've sent it out to anyone who wants it," Peace said.

"How many UFOs have you seen?"

"Well, all told, from that first one I saw in Portland flying over Reed's campus, I figure this is about fifty."

Seriously? I thought. *Fifty UFOs?*

"Most people aren't open to the idea of alien portals," she said, "but something is happening now. I've seen more UFOs in the last year than I'd seen in the prior twenty-five years of my life. I know some people believe that the vibrations are changing between this physical world that you and I experience," she said as she grabbed my hand for emphasis, "and the spirit world. Messages are coming from all over, and people are beginning to sense the change."

"What do you think is going to happen, Peace?"

"I don't know yet," she said, "but I'm making a list of people who have some kind of power or gifts, and I'd like to put you on it."

"Me?" I asked.

"You don't see it yet, but you've got something. I can feel it."

"You think it's the end of the world?" I asked, getting uncomfortable about everything.

"No," she said and smiled. "I think it's the beginning."

Chapter 20
Goodbye

THE ANSWER TO THE QUESTION about trust came from a place that I didn't expect.

Rebecca, Hugh's editor, Kayla, and I were carrying Hugh's ashes, ready to construct a medicine wheel where Hugh and I had hiked to the Wallow Canyon Vortex. I'd given Kayla back her Jeep and thanked her for it. The day was warm and the red rock contrasted with the powder-blue sky in a color combination that could have come from an artist. Clouds moved by and blocked the sun, but only temporarily, and again the heat from the sun's energy, masculine energy, touched the female energy of the earth. This is how the natives believe that man came to be—from the conception of the sun's masculine energy united with the earth's female energy.

I thought about this belief as we set the ashes to the wind. The life cycle of anything—be it a beloved pet, a mother, father, sister, brother, husband, or even the shortest of relationships moves in a circle of beginning, middle, and end. When a relationship is over, then growth occurs. It happens through a death, or through distance, or through the way people change, but it always happens.

In a marriage, sometimes it happens before the death part. There is a life to relationships. The hardest part is knowing when to walk away from one.

At this point, with hindsight, I knew this with Danny. Was there a reason why he'd come into my life's path?

We'd taken rocks and formed the outside of the circle of the wheel. Marker rocks, larger than the others, formed the four directions. South was toward intuition and trust to uncover the nature of one's heart, west was toward introspection and looking within with reflection, east was the illumination toward clear vision, and north expanded the gift of wisdom. In the middle we made a birth spot where every aspect of a person was believed to be known. Truly, I was in Sedona to learn and grow and heal and become who I was meant to be. Even from these events, it was as it should be.

As we spread the ashes of Hugh, I felt a joyful song emerge within me; it was one I had never known before and one that I had sung at different times in my life; it transcended the moment and time and place and turned inward toward my animal guide—the bear—a symbol of power and strength and courage; it was a medicine healer with curative power who walked with me. I knew this from my time in the sweat lodge and my soul retrieval.

I watched the ceremony and looked to the east—the portal for creating a new vision for life—and saw the hummingbird, also my spirit guide. I realized there had been many times when I would see the hummingbird and report my discovery to Aunt Thelma. She told me that I was the hummingbird—that I, like that totem animal, spread inner joy and love to those I meet; that I am able to find the good in people, and that it searches for the sweetness in life and in the plant—often moving past the tough, bitter part to reach the sweet essence of the flower, or the love within a person.

And finally, I felt the presence of the deer, barely discernible in the distance from the vortex, a spirit that is swift and alert but also intuitive, with grace, balance, and gratitude. At that time the anger slipped from me, and I felt the negative energy, transmuted, go back into the earth.

I looked around this medicine wheel, and I vowed, in this lifetime, to take the time to express my appreciation to those who had touched me in some way in my life, to affirm it to those who, even for a brief time in my life, made it better. I vowed not to wait until a wake or funeral or any kind of memorial to offer the words, but to express it even at the expense of my own vulnerability.

As we left, I told Rebecca I'd be along in a few minutes. I needed a little more time to understand why all three of my animal guides had appeared. For I recognized it was an extraordinary event even as I said goodbye to Hugh's spirit and turned toward the east as a portal for the changes that were pulling me toward a new life. My time in Sedona was coming to an end. I had a new direction to take, and though I wasn't quite sure where that would be, I knew enough and felt enough, and my intuitiveness had developed enough, that Sedona was only a part of my future for a little while longer.

I felt a presence behind me. At first I thought that Rebecca had come back—that perhaps I'd completely lost track of the time—but when I turned around, I saw the form of Kuruk standing with me.

I was not dream traveling this time. I was physically present in the moment at this vortex with an energy running through me that began where my shoes touched the red rocks. And Kuruk was not in spirit form.

"Have you been here all the time?" I asked as I turned toward the age-etched face of the old medicine man.

"Yes."

"Why did you come?"

He pointed toward the north. "His spirit needs to leave. Navajos believe we must not show emotion so the dead cannot be distracted from the other world or they will want to remain. It is his time to go."

We looked north and saw the buck mule deer turn toward us, eyes transfixed, caught by light. It turned, blended into the surroundings, and was gone.

I said to Kuruk after Hugh's spirit had gone, "I forgave Danny today. I let my anger go, and I've returned to the balance in my inner self."

"Everything is not as it appears."

"Wait!" I said to Kuruk. "What isn't as it appears?"

"Watch the signs. They are all around us." He started down the trail, walking slowly, medicine stick in hand.

I looked where Hugh's spirit had disappeared. "Goodbye, Hugh," I said as I walked the trail to meet the others.

When I got back to the trailhead, I asked Rebecca if she had seen Kuruk.

"You couldn't have missed him," I said. "Navajo medicine man with a walking stick, a little bent over with age."

"No one has come down the trail, Lizzy."

Maybe he took another way back, I thought. But I hadn't noticed another way.

I decided to let it go. *At least for now.*

Chapter 21
Kachina Woman

WE WERE IN THE MIDST of rehearsal for *Romeo and Juliet* when Ryan came up and threw a big hug around me. He'd been released on bail. He was gaunt, but otherwise he didn't look too bad. Certainly not completely out of the hands of the legal system, but we were at least at a point where he could begin working again. The check problem was attributed to a deposit that was put into the wrong account. I'd been reimbursed for the money I'd given Simon. So everything should have been back in balance. Except for me, that didn't happen. And I couldn't figure out why. I kept thinking back to what Kuruk had said about the signs, but the only signs I could see were that things were moving forward. Everything, that is, except my divorce.

In the realm of the legal system, I now had the oldest unresolved domestic suit on file for Multnomah County, Portland, Oregon, where my attorney had filed it. Somehow, that wasn't a record I was excited to keep. I'd spin through my options, but when I called the attorney, I encountered higher bills and nothing changed. So I'd try to forget the situation until something reminded me of it and I'd spin through the same conversation again with the attorney.

I pushed through with painting backgrounds for the next season, even though I felt I wasn't going to be in Sedona much longer and wouldn't be able to enjoy seeing my creativity in the production. I hadn't said anything to anyone yet, but I knew.

I'd called to check on Aunt Thelma again to give her the good news about Ryan's bail and the sense of normalcy the theater was regaining, but the grip of her dementia was firmly in place and unwilling to let go. Each time I called I was hopeful, and each time I'd get the same report that she didn't know or remember anything connected with her past. I'd talk to her for a while, but usually I was met with silence or confusion. It was frustrating. Emotionally it was draining. But each time I hoped she would remember.

I wasn't looking for trouble, but something kept nagging at my intuition. So I planned to visit Boynton Canyon, not far from Sedona, on my Monday off from work.

It was considered a major vortex for balancing masculine and feminine energy. I'd planned to visit it when I'd first gotten to Sedona, but events had prevented it. Now seemed to be the time to draw upon its balance.

I expected to be gone for a good part of the day. Water, sunscreen, sunglasses, cell phone, and a snack bag of almonds were in my day pack. Boynton Canyon had been, in times past, inhabited by the Apache and Yavapai Indians. It is believed that through the centuries the Navajo, Hopi, and Zuni also inhabited it. About nine hundred years ago, the Sinagua tribe abandoned its cliff dwellings in the canyon. To the Apache, the canyon is where First Woman Spirit came to the people and taught the races of the world's cultures how to use the colors of the kernels of corn, and it is believed by the Apache that Spirit will come again. The first time she appeared it was after the great flood; scientists determined—from the striated layers of rock—that Boynton Canyon was indeed at one time underwater. And to add to the mystic nature of the canyon, a tribe called themselves the dolphin people.

The vortex at Boynton Canyon was reported, in oral tradition, by the Aborigine people of Australia, to be a spiritual place. Dream travelers identified the site in Sedona as sacred.

The Kachina Woman Knoll, a hot spot of the vortex activity, was my destination. Since I'd started out fairly early, it was still cool. I thought about the balance: Masculine energy to take charge of my life—standing up to people who try to take it away by intimidation, taking appropriate risks, and my ability to reason without distorting reality. The feminine energy from the vortex was to assist me in kindness, compassion, considerateness, and the ability to anticipate my impact on others.

I need both. Everyone needs both.

It was an easy hike, and I met a few people along the trail before I reached the knoll of Kachina Woman and stopped to see if I could feel the psychometer, as Aunt Thelma had called it in her book—the vibration where I could feel the tingling sensation that would start in my toes and head up my legs.

Part of all this was to quiet myself. Pushing away the mental churning that distracts from what a person can feel or see or sense, I was distracted by my own mental activity. It was about Danny. And it kept coming back to Danny. And then I'd clear him out of my head—actually, I yelled at him to get out of it—and then he'd slip into it again.

I needed to get physical in order to push him out of my psyche. I tried a tree pose as I stood in the middle of the vortex; I brought my hands up over my heart chakra and stretched my hands over my head, turning my palms outward, and returned my hands to my heart again. After several times in that pose, I switched to the right side and repeated it.

And as soon as I was done, Danny's smile popped into my head again. *This is ridiculous,* I thought. *Why can't I let this go?*

I tried a few more poses, and each time I'd be able to center myself, but then the image of Danny would come back front and center into my brain. It's really painful to break up from a serious encounter post-divorce (in my case it was post-separation).

I decided that I couldn't gain much benefit from any kind of vortex energy when I was in such a state of post-relationship churning. I shrugged and grabbed my day pack and headed back to the car.

The sky was beginning to clear. Making good time descending the trail, I got back to my car and dropped my pack on the passenger side of the car and drank a few deep gulps of water. Getting into the driver's side and turning the ignition, I decided I'd drop by the *Sedona Red Rock News* and see what Rebecca had found out about Matthew Bell's fire. Investigators were to make a determination about it today. I was curious to know if the police had any new leads on Nicole's and Hugh's deaths.

Driving back, I almost had Danny pushed out of my mind when I saw a car behind me—moving a lot faster than it should be—hit me from behind.

Kabam! The sound of metal hitting metal and the crunch of breaking glass permeated the air. The other car backed off, and I was ready to do my civic duty to exchange information when I looked into the rearview mirror to see the vehicle speeding up to ram me again. *Holy crap,* I thought as I did a quick maneuver back to the road. The problem was that this road by Boynton Canyon was pretty desolate, and I wasn't sure where I'd be able to get help. And the driver of the beater-type car, which I recognized as the late-model

Chevy from Cottonwood, was driven by the sleazeball beer guzzler who had tried to hurt me in Nicole's apartment.

I tried a quick turn toward a patch of road where the desert and the road weren't all that distinct from one another. *Why is he trying to hurt me?*

Trying to save myself, I punched on the accelerator and inched up on the speedometer to the maximum in the Subaru, which wasn't saying a whole hell of a lot. *Great,* I thought, *I'm toast.*

The Chevy rammed me again, harder this time, and we connected with a screech and a mash of metal. I floored the accelerator, all the while trying desperately to think of some kind of plan.

I'd managed to make it into the outskirts of Sedona. The creep was still behind, ready to ram me again. I had my foot to the floor with the accelerator but couldn't go any faster. With nothing more to do than try to control the car from careening off the road, I had to think of something. But when I looked back again, I saw smoke inexplicably barrel up from the Chevy. Just before that I'd heard a strange sound. I'd never heard anything like it before. I eased off the pedal and looked at a spectacular car fire behind me.

I floored the accelerator again to get away. In a final burst of power, the car pulled away from the smoking Chevy, until all I could see was a dot like a lit cigarette on the highway. By this time, I could feel my heart pound and every pore in my body released adrenaline. My hands shook as I navigated toward the Sedona Justice Center. I pulled into the parking lot and ran inside, heart still pounding.

The cop at the desk did a double take. I took a deep breath and asked for Officer J. Hall.

He came around the corner, took one look at me, and knew to take me back to his workstation where he offered me some water or coffee to drink. I took the water.

"I thought you liked the coffee here," he quipped.

"Someone's trying to kill me," I said, "and I'm getting tired of it."

He looked at me with deep concern. "Tell me about it."

"These guys from Cottonwood," I said, "are really annoying me." Hall shuffled through his files on his desk and pulled out some photographs.

"Would any of these guys be the ones?"

I spotted the creep from his photograph with his picked-on face and missing teeth. "That's the guy," I said and then excused myself to go to the restroom where I threw up, wrenching with the contents of my breakfast floating in the toilet bowl. I went to the sink and washed out the nastiness in my mouth. The water tasted sweet. Splashing cold water on my face, I looked in the mirror at my reflection. "What the hell is going on?" I said to the image.

When I got back to his workstation, Hall told me he had sent a police cruiser to investigate. It didn't take very long before a call came back that a burned-out Chevy was, indeed, on the side of the highway as I described it and was being towed to the station. I'd given them the rest of the information, including the address of the sleazeballs in Cottonwood, but I expected that the creeps would probably be south of the border in no time at all. Hall walked me to my Subaru, now looking more like a mini cruiser since it had been smashed in, and took photographs to add to the report.

"It still drives?" he asked.

Chapter 22

Forgiveness

AT TIMES LIKE THIS, IN the everyday existence of humanity, it's difficult to understand when the spirit world speaks. I'd done what I had to do and reported to the police. That was a hard knock on my dignity. Now I had to make peace with whatever it was that was pulling me in so many directions. Without acknowledging it, I didn't know if I'd survive.

Hall knew I was afraid. "Do me a favor," he said as he opened the driver's-side car door for me. "Be careful."

I looked up at his exquisite blue eyes and softened.

"I'll try," I said.

I drove my car up the winding road that leads to the Holy Chapel of the Cross on Chapel Road in Sedona. The last part of the drive is up a spiral of roadway that takes on the most spectacular view. But the best part is inside the church because it was built, as if suspended, over the cliffs. It is a perfect place for meditation, reflection, and alms-giving.

I was told when I'd moved to Sedona that a person has to have her karma in order to be able to live there. People who couldn't get that balance had to leave—some moving to Cottonwood to avoid the karmic energy. Whether I believed it or not, I was here to make amends. It was time to give up the part of my past that was taking too much of my energy in the negative. I was here to make peace.

Spiritualists, like my Aunt Thelma, believe that people feel the increased vibrations as we plow ahead in the century. All I knew is that it was time to let go of the negativity that I held—either emotionally or financially. *And what better place*, I thought, *than the Catholic church in Sedona?*

I'd been to mass with my dad and struggled with the sacraments but was encouraged to go through the motions. I'd been attracted to my estranged husband because I thought he was like my father, but now, like true knowledge illuminated, I knew that it was what I wanted to see in him. He was nothing like my dad.

I genuflected at the stone pew as a sign of respect. I gave it all up to Spirit in the Chapel of the Cross. Rising, I went to the devotional candles and lit one for Hugh, I lit one for Nicole, and I lit one for my Aunt Thelma, who I knew was soon to pass. I figured wherever the prayers and intentions and love goes, it doesn't really matter what the religion.

I walked out with a sense that I was a better person for it. But I had one more thing I had to do. I sat on a bench outside the church with a commanding view of the red-rock desert. I turned on my cell phone and placed the call to my Uncle Callaghan.

"Law Offices of Callaghan, Fagan, and Mohan."

"John Callaghan, please," I asked.

"Who's calling, please?"

"Tell him it's his niece," I said. There was dead air.

"Lizzy," Uncle Callaghan said when he picked up the telephone.

I tried to compose myself. I heard him clearing his throat on the other end of the line. After we got our emotions in check he said, "Is there anything I can do?"

I think he meant about life in general. But I took the time to explain the events in Sedona. He promised to call Ryan. He had not accepted his "coming out" in the past, but now he wanted to make amends.

"I know," I added at the end of the conversation, "that you're busy, but I have another favor. I need some help to finish this divorce. That's the way you can help me."

"Of course," he said. "I'll look into it."

I knew if anyone could get something taken care of, it was my Uncle Callaghan.

Chapter 23

The Cheaters

THERE'S ALWAYS A MOTIVATION FOR human behavior. All I had to do was find the missing piece of the puzzle. Rebecca and I were meeting at the Coffee Pot Restaurant. I ordered the number thirty-three, the quintessential omelet: avocado, bacon, onions, tomato, and cheese. It wasn't a death wish. It was comfort food.

We sat in a booth and drank coffee while our waitress took the order.

Rebecca also succumbed to the pleasure of the number thirty-three omelet. I was beginning to warm up to her change in palette. Maybe surviving in a mine for thirty-six hours made her rethink her bird diet.

"Well," she said, "Matthew Bell's house might have been arson."

Our conversation switched when the waitress brought the omelets to the table with biscuits and hash browns.

"I'm going to the art festival after we eat," I told Rebecca. "I'm buying something for my Aunt Thelma. Do you want to come along?"

"Sure," Rebecca agreed. "I've acquired your taste for retail therapy."

When we reached the gates of the festival, it smelled of barbeque. The sky radiated a brilliant sapphire blue. We'd shopped for about an hour, but I still hadn't found anything special for my aunt, so we bought two lemonades.

There were still several more booths to explore. I was distracted with shopping when Rebecca looked up from her lemonade and asked, "Isn't that Matthew Bell over there?"

It sure was Matthew. I watched as he took his iPhone through numerous applications.

My jaw dropped. I stammered something nonsensical because as I watched, Louise Smith joined him and they kissed. It wasn't a friendly little peck-on-the-cheek kiss; it was a passionate, full-blown, mouth-to-mouth kiss. I grabbed Rebecca by the shirtsleeve and pulled her behind a booth selling Sedona art.

"Holy, crap," I whispered to Rebecca, "Matthew is cheating on Ryan with Louise!"

This didn't look good.

"Once a cheater, always a cheater," Rebecca hissed.

"My relationship hangover just took a nosedive," I said to Rebecca.

"More importantly, Lizzy," Rebecca said as we both skulked to another booth where we couldn't be observed, "could your intuitive anxiousness be about this?"

"I don't know," I whispered to Rebecca. "Let's follow them and see where they go."

Sleuthing is not as easy as it looks. We had a lot of people around us; one slip-up and we'd be recognized for sure. I remembered that I still had the blonde wig and theater makeup in my car. I'd planned to return everything to the greenhouse office, but I hadn't gotten around to it yet.

Rebecca continued to watch the couple. Their passionate embrace had terminated, and they actually appeared nervous at their indiscretion. I went back to my car and took out the box with the makeup and wig. The wig wasn't in great shape after everything I'd been through in the mine, but I pulled my brush out of my bag and frantically combed the hair until it looked halfway presentable. Using my rearview mirror, I adjusted the wig on my head and gave it a few more brushstrokes—just for good measure.

I took the makeup from the bag and went with the red lipstick and the drama of blue shadow and eyeliner. Viola! I looked like Marilyn Monroe again. I took a black linen scarf I'd planned to donate to the costume box and wrapped it around my neck in a convincing fashion statement. I had a new persona.

Making my way back to the section of booths occupied by artists, I called Rebecca with my cell phone. By the time I'd caught up with her, she was surprised when she turned around to see me.

"Gosh," she said, "great disguise."

"I'm going to follow them. Give me your car keys."

Rebecca said, "I'm supposed to hand over my BMW to you?"

She had a point. A new BMW was not much of an exchange for a Subaru with over 125 thousand miles on it and a smashed rear-end that made it look like a pug cruiser.

"Here," I said as I handed over my keys, "you'll get the exclusive."

"I'm only doing this because you saved me in the mine," she said. "I don't usually let anyone drive my car."

The deal was sealed. In faux Marilyn Monroe attire, I got into her BMW. It smelled like a new car, and I inhaled deeply. I was a blonde with a hot car—my wildest dreams come true.

"Do you know how to drive a stick shift?" Rebecca asked me through the window, a hint of despair rising in her voice as I engaged the clutch and popped the car into reverse.

"I'm going to get your car back to you safe and sound," I lied.

A new BMW with a tight clutch was the least of my worries.

Matthew and Louise were making good time in his Mercedes. What I had going for me was that they stopped at every light to make out. *Get a room.* I'd grown tired of their public displays of affection. Drumming my fingers on the steering wheel, I couldn't get out of my mind how Ryan would feel when I told him.

The Mercedes pulled out as the light turned green, and I was able to handle the clutch without calling attention to myself. They were headed south, and I kept enough distance that they didn't suspect—or I hoped that they didn't suspect—that a hot blonde in a BMW was actually following them. I realized I was in for a longer trip than I'd planned because the Mercedes continued to head south toward Cottonwood. *Why are they headed there? Does Louise live in Cottonwood?*

I wondered how I would tell Ryan of Matthew's infidelity. My thoughts were interrupted by my cell phone. It was Rebecca.

"Is my car still in one piece?" she asked.

"Of course," I said, "and you're not going to believe where I'm headed."

I told her that Cottonwood appeared to be the destination of the tryst. Cottonwood appeared to be the epicenter of everything. I passed the apartment complex where I'd had my run-in with the scumbags.

When the Mercedes finally stopped, we were in a housing development of five- to seven-million-dollar homes. Louise and

Matthew got out of the car and went into an expensive one. I was confident they couldn't see me from where I'd stopped, but I was grateful I had the disguise. The time ticked by while I waited, and the car was getting hot. I looked around for something to drink. I found a half-stick of gum in the glove box and chewed on it. That made me even thirstier. I consoled myself with the knowledge that Louise had a performance tonight and sooner or later she'd come out.

After an hour, they did. I was flushed with heat. The two lovebirds got back in the Mercedes and turned into a McDonald's drive-through window. I waited. On Sixth Street they turned toward a public storage building. I parked in a slice of shade and got out to follow on foot.

By the time I'd gotten around a corner, I caught a view of them at the door of a storage unit building with the Mercedes still idling. I had to do everything I could to withhold an audible gasp—because there stood Matthew and Louise and the two creeps who had turned my Subaru into a MINI Cooper. I'd figured the drug-hazed, sleazeball men would have been out of the country by now—at least out of Cottonwood—but something gave them a stronger reason to stay, and I was about ready to find out.

I saw the deal as the drugs changed hands, but I wasn't the only one watching the illegal activity because I heard someone yell at them to put their hands in the air. Next thing I knew, shots exploded like fireworks. Louise was firing shots and managed to run. Cops appeared out of nowhere and started to shoot.

Shit, I thought as people splayed behind cars, doorways, and anywhere else to find cover from bullets. *Ping, ping.*

I skulked backward toward the BMW. *I need to get out of here.* Tires squealed rubber in the distance. I ran toward the BMW and was dialing the police from my cell phone when I saw the barrel of a gun pointed at my blonde wig.

It was Louise. She grabbed my cell phone out of my hand and crushed it under her boot. I regretted the day I'd suggested to Ryan that she take Nicole's job. I felt like I'd been a pawn. I never liked to lose at a game of chess. And while I was in check, it wasn't checkmate yet.

"Get out of the car, Lizzy," Louise ordered me.

"You saw through the disguise?"

She snorted. "You're a royal pain in the ass."

I was angry that I hadn't figured Louise to be at the epicenter of Ryan's crisis and mad that she'd wrecked my cell phone.

"I figured you and Matthew wanted Nicole dead. Was it drugs, or work, or was it both?" I asked.

Louise laughed. "Nicole was stupid," she said. "Everyone is replaceable. Right now, I want the car."

Sweat prickled my back. *Checkmate.*

I was thinking about Catholic last rites as I saw a car careen toward us at full speed. A premonition in full force, I took a leap of faith and jumped onto the hood of the BMW, rolled, and ducked toward the other side of the car. Louise, apparently, was too startled to react. I heard a *thump* and watched as Louise's body flew up into the air like a rag doll. The impact left her boots on the hot asphalt—yards from where her body made contact with the road. Metal against metal crunched as the BMW shuddered at the impact of the sideswiping car. The errant automobile ran over Louise's body and disappeared up the street.

The Cottonwood police chalked around the body and gathered statements from the witnesses. There weren't many. I drove

Rebecca's BMW back to Sedona. I knew she was going to be mad about the car. But what I realized is that I'd seen the car that careened down the street and killed Louise. I needed to make a trip to Navajo land.

Driving north again toward the reservation, I replayed the telephone call I'd made to Ryan when I'd gotten back to my apartment. I gave him the news about Louise and about Matthew, who hadn't made it through the shoot-out. With both gone, I wasn't sure what he'd say, but the strength of my brother—especially in the wake of broken relationships—amazed me. He had a philosophy on life and death that was reserved for the most elder of a tribe, and in his acceptance of his own sexuality, he forgave.

It wasn't going to be without a relationship hangover, but he'd be okay, and I believed he'd thrive. Kayla offered to take the lead for the duration of the performance. The theater would finish the season in a few weeks, and receipts continued on an upturn.

Using memory and natural points of reference—albeit two wrong turns, since my sense of direction has never been the best—I made my way to the unmarked mileage post and turned down the dusty road toward Lynea's hogan. It was the summer solstice in Arizona—it would be dark at eight o'clock—and I hoped to get there before the last light.

In my own way, I knew she was aware of my coming. In the keen sense of anyone who is connected and listening to a higher power—be it as a developing intuitive or as a healer or a teacher—Lynea knew that I would recognize the car that saved my life by leveling it at Louise. My premonition prior to her coming down that road was that I was living the hand that was dealt.

Zeek came to the car and sniffed, and then he sat down for his treat. I'd anticipated this and filled my pocket with several of Karma's treats before I left my apartment.

Lynea walked out the front door of the hogan—a halo of the interior light cast around her like the sacred geometry of her spirit guides—and smiled.

"I was expecting you sooner, Lizzy," she said.

"The police took a long time in Cottonwood, and then I had to call Ryan about Matthew and Louise," I replied. "Of course, I told the police that I'd never seen the car before."

Lynea smiled. "It was Kuruk's vision."

Lynea explained about the drugs on the reservation. She'd watched two of her brightest students die last year. Tonight, thanks to Lynea, there were a few less drugs in the hands of kids—at least for a while. I knew that someone else would take their place.

"Are you going to turn me in?" Lynea asked. I was struck with the moral conflict similar to *Huckleberry Finn*. The main character, Huck, struggled with his decision to turn in Jim, a slave, who was also his friend. It was against the law to harbor a slave. Huck knew it. But he realized in the middle of that river that he couldn't turn in his friend. He decided to break the law and face hell instead. I was faced with the same kind of ethical dilemma. I decided to face hell, too.

"No," I told Lynea.

Chapter 24
Leaving

WHILE GOING THROUGH A RELATIONSHIP hangover, it's a good idea to keep plenty of aspirin around, along with Bloody Mary mix and vodka. In the morning it can help head off the next wave of the hangover. I wanted something to take away the residual waves of emotion that I was riding. Tempted to call Officer J. Hall, I reconsidered. Cops had not been good for me. I told myself not to let his blue eyes or buff body get the better of me. I'd spend some time with myself and figure out the nature of my mistakes before I repeated them again.

I set about to do the right thing with Rebecca and her smashed BMW. Like the Navajo's the Blessing Way song—used to apologize for any slights known or unknown—it was time for me to do the same. Rebecca didn't take the news of the car well. But when she heard the full accounting—minus the information about Lynea—she forgave me. She had an exclusive interview and figured she'd finish the feature series that Hugh had started. Maybe it was Rebecca who'd end up with a choice job at the *New York Times*.

A feature article appeared in the *Sedona Red Rock News* that detailed the drug ring, a full accounting of the killers back and forth movement across the border, Louise's alleged involvement and connections to the drug culture (which, it turns out, is how she originally met Nicole Preston), and Matthew's interest in the lucrative and fast-cash part of the business.

It was when Nicole began to blackmail Matthew—she threatened to tell Ryan about Louise and Matthew's relationship—that Louise had devised the plan to lure Nicole to the medicine wheel where Matthew and Louise killed Nicole. It was easy to frame Ryan because Louise knew of the public argument at the theater.

Louise had worked at the theater with Nicole in Ashland, and it was gossiped that Nicole had started the fire in the theater—but it was Louise's idea to burn Matthew's Sedona house to help finance the seven-million-dollar home in Cottonwood. Apparently, Matthew and Louise couldn't handle the karma in Sedona, like so many residents report—if their karma wasn't in balance, people moved to Cottonwood. But since Matthew couldn't sell the house fast enough, he'd taken to Louise's suggestion to start the fire for the insurance money. Matthew died from a bullet from the shoot-out in Cottonwood; he'd lived for a few hours, was rushed to the Verde Valley Medical Center, and never regained consciousness. One of the scumbag drug dealer smugglers disappeared during the mayhem—presumably he'd made his way across the border again to Mexico—and the police were looking for him, along with Nicole's former boyfriend, Dave Lewis. The other scumbag died in the shoot-out.

Two Cottonwood police officers had been killed. A memorial was to be held in Cottonwood later.

I'd let Ryan know that I'd be leaving as stage manager after we wrapped up the summer season. He tried to talk me into staying, but after a few weak arguments, he shrugged and gave up because he knew me well enough to know that I'd made up my mind and there was no changing my course. Kayla agreed to take over in my position; she said she wanted to save as much money as possible for the wedding with her boyfriend. I still hadn't told her about the four kids and the white picket fence, but she also hadn't asked me for any more details about what her future held, so I figured she wanted to go along for life's ride and see where it took her. And I wanted to try to get my life back on track.

I'd tried several times to talk to Aunt Thelma, but the reports each time were that she was slipping further into the grips of Alzheimer's. I planned to head back to Portland to see her.

Lynea started to say something about Danny, but I cut her off because it was a wound too fresh for me.

When Rebecca came to the door, I was in my apartment packing boxes.

"Want some help?" she offered.

"Sure."

We were in the middle of the living room with a column of boxes I'd picked up from the grocery store before they'd been recycled.

"Are you sure you want to leave?" Rebecca asked. "You've made friends."

I tried to find the words to convey that something was driving me forward on a path I didn't know, but a path I had to take it. However, something was still out of balance. The night before, in my dreams, a rat clamped down on my hand with its glistening yellow teeth. I woke up in a sweat.

We packed my mishmash of dishes and most of my clothes. I packed away an amulet I'd purchased for Aunt Thelma. I bought her a quartz wand to assist her memory and help her healing. I'd wrapped it in tissue and tucked it into my bag to give her as soon as I got back to Portland. Driving with a smashed-in Subaru wasn't the way I'd expected to return, but I figured I'd scrape together enough to buy something with the insurance money after that was settled. Rebecca asked about packing Aunt Thelma's books, and I told her I'd wait until last to do that.

She was thrilled about the accolades she'd received regarding her feature article. As I sat across from her, I felt that her time in the Southwest was also about to come to an end. She'd be headed for New York and a new life.

"What's your plan when you're in New York? Do you want a visitor?"

Rebecca looked surprised. "Is this intuition?"

"It doesn't take an intuitive to know you're on to bigger things," I told her.

She grinned. "I've always imagined myself in New York."

We made a quick errand to the cell phone store on L'Auberge Lane. I told the same woman who had helped me before that I needed to replace my cell phone.

"Let me see," she said, "you drove off the cliff again?"

"No," I said. "That would be a ridiculous story. Actually, this time it was smashed by someone who wanted to steal my friend's BMW. And now that person is dead."

"Tell you what," the clerk said, "I'll give you a replacement for free."

It was time to pack Aunt Thelma's books. With each book I sensed something, but no magic instructions came to mind. If I'd missed an important message, it was in front of me, but I couldn't decipher it.

My telephone rang. "Lizzy," Uncle Callaghan began, "your attorney and I about have this thing wrapped up. Opposing counsel doesn't want to go to trial. When we put the screws to him, he decided it was time to settle."

Maybe this was going to be a good day.

Callaghan cleared his throat and continued, "Your attorney hired a private investigator and discovered your husband had numerous relationships with prostitutes. We have photographs. He didn't want to have to explain his weakness to a Multnomah County judge. We've been able to negotiate a better settlement, and I think you'll be pleased. Of course," Callaghan added, "he wants the facts and information about the sex-for-money kept quiet. My advice to you is to settle and be done with the asshole. Take the high road and let it go."

Chapter 25
Final Act

WHILE UNCLE CALLAGHAN HAD HELPED my legal and financial situation, the fact that I'd found out how emotionally corrupt my estranged husband was had launched another emotional hangover.

I figured some yoga might help me to feel better. Or a gallon of ice cream.

Maybe both. However, I looked at my watch and knew I'd have to get to the kiosk for ticket sales. I also planned to stay after the performance and clean out the office and get ready to finish up what I needed to do there. My need to leave Sedona grew.

There was a line of people when I arrived at the kiosk, so I didn't have time to get anything done before the performance. As I was selling tickets, I looked up, after I'd sold to a group of seniors who qualified for a discount, to see a tanned, blue-eyed off-duty police officer in line.

"Officer J. Hall," I said. "Finally ready to see the show?"

"Yes," he said. His blue eyes looked intense. "And could I convince you to have dinner with me afterward?"

It was a nice offer. But I'd sworn off dating for a while. "I planned to work after the show," I answered.

"I'll wait," he said.

What do I really have to lose? I asked myself. I had to eat, and I couldn't go back to my apartment of boxes without having something. I didn't have anything left in the refrigerator except a box of soda to keep the smell away. And I was about to leave Sedona anyway.

"Okay," I agreed, "but something quick. Then I can come back and get some work done." I called out, "By the way, what's your first name, Officer J. Hall? I like to know a man's first name before I go out to dinner with him."

"It's John," he answered.

John Hall drove me in his Lexus to Cucina Rustica on 179. The dark encapsulated the night punctuated with bright stars as we were led to the outside seating with lighting that spotlighted the red-rock views.

I ordered the grilled prawns wrapped in prosciutto with a lemon-basil cream. Hall ordered the steak with the roasted potatoes and each of us ordered a glass of wine. My self talk started out something like this: *Lizzy, don't have too much wine because you have work at the theater after dinner. But,* I think, *I have to eat.* It goes like that with the self talk: the pros and cons and then I usually default to whatever I was doing in the first place. And right now I was sitting across the table from a ticket-giving nemesis who had evolved to a dinner date.

"Why did you ask me out?" I asked as I devoured a grilled prawn. I wanted to sigh with the flavors on my tongue, but knew it was bad manners to get that worked up over shellfish on a first date.

"You're interesting," he answered.

I've been called a lot of things in my life, but interesting usually wasn't in the lineup.

"I'm leaving at the end of the week," I said as I took a sip of chardonnay and jabbed another prawn on my fork.

He had no idea. "You're free to do that," he said like a cop, "but would you reconsider?"

We'd been through this little dance in my kitchen when he went in for the kiss—which shouldn't have happened in the first place.

"I have to go back and get the divorce finished—to sign the papers. And my Aunt Thelma's health is getting worse, so I need to spend time with her."

He played with the food in front of him. "Something has troubled me…"

Something was bothering me, too. But the flavor of the prawns washed down with the chardonnay made all my other cares go away. *Oh,* I thought. *Be careful. You don't want to end up in the backseat with this guy.*

"It's about Cottonwood," he said.

I tossed back the rest of the wine and caught the waiter's eye. I hoped Hall wasn't going to dig into what I was withholding. I'd take Lynea's secret to my grave.

"It doesn't add up," he said. "Matthew and Louise wanted to frame Ryan, but why were the others hell-bent after you?"

A good question, and it was at the center of my consciousness. I remembered what happened in Nicole's apartment and everything else. It wasn't tidy.

"I thought tonight was a date," I said to steer the conversation away from Cottonwood and my nebulous premonitions.

He said, "It's hard for me to quit thinking about cases some-times." With that he took his glass in hand: "I propose that we change the subject."

We tapped glasses with a *chink*.

"Here's to us," he said.

Dessert was a killer chocolate mousse.

Back to the theater to finish up my chores, Hall walked me to the door of the greenhouse office. As I said goodnight, he leaned in for the kiss that I'd blocked before. And when he kissed me, I felt a surge of energy unlike anything I'd felt before. My legs went weak underneath me.

Holy cow, I thought. *I've never been kissed like that before.* I felt like a melted Hersey's chocolate.

I moaned and came up for air.

It's really not fair that a police officer can kiss like that, I thought. I'd sworn off dating, I'd definitely sworn off cops, and I was hell-bent to leave Sedona. *And now I get kissed like this?*

Chapter 26
Leaving Sedona

I SORTED THROUGH THE MOUNDS of paperwork in the office. Working through the receipts, I got the deposit ready. Some costumes needed to go to the dry cleaners, so I set everything by the door. All in all, things were looking pretty good. And it was close to midnight. I decided it was time to head back to the apartment. The trouble was what my premonition had activated. But between the wine and the kiss, I wasn't really tuned into it until I realized I was rubbing my eyes because of a twitch.

I was just tired, I tried to convince myself.

I considered calling Hall. He'd given me his card, and he'd written his cell number on it. *No.* That kiss was dangerous. If I called him again, I'm not sure what I'd do in my activated hormonal state.

I decided since I hadn't gone into full-blown premonition, I'd gather up what I had by the door and leave with my cell phone in my pocket and keys in my hand. I'd get in a good jab at something if someone was out there.

It was well lit where I was parked. I figured a few people would still be out and about nearby with the restaurant bars still open.

I made a backup plan, so I could run into one of those establishments; I walked with purpose.

When I got to my car and unlocked the door, I thought I was home free. I put the costumes into the back and jumped into the front seat. I looked around and didn't see anything. I took a check of my senses. Whatever I'd felt at the greenhouse office had disappeared.

I shrugged and put the car in reverse. I rubbed at my twitching eye.

At home, Karma reluctantly removed herself from the warm nest she'd made on the couch while I was gone. I took her out to relieve herself, and we were back in the apartment in a matter of minutes.

I flipped on the bathroom light and looked at myself in the mirror. Actually, I looked better than I had in the last year. That underscored how awful the last year had been for me.

I brushed my teeth, flossed, washed my face, and added a spot of age-defying cream to the corners of my eyes. I pulled on an oversized shirt and crawled into bed. Pulling the covers to my chin, I felt Karma plop next to the bed and release a huge sigh. Before a few minutes had passed, she twitched as she dreamed of chasing tennis balls, or rabbits, or whatever it is that dogs chase in dreams.

That wine I'd had at dinner gave me a headache. I'd taken a couple aspirin.

Tossing and turning, I watched the digital alarm clock turn to yet a later hour of the night, so I decided to take one of the sleeping pills my doctor had prescribed for me when I'd first come upon my copulating husband.

The red numerals glowed three o'clock.

I heard a sharp crack of breaking glass from my living room.

Why didn't Karma bark? Still in the haze of the pill, I tried to pull my thoughts together. *If Karma didn't bark, did I imagine it?*

I grabbed my terrycloth bathrobe from the bottom of my bed and wrapped it around me and tied it with a yank. I strained to listen.

Taking my cell phone from my nightstand, I crept into the living room and felt broken glass on my bare feet. I looked up and saw a gaping hole from the smashed-out living room window.

Oh no, I thought, *I didn't imagine it.*

I punched the buttons for 911, but before I could finish the call, I felt a sharp pain explode in the middle of my back from a karate kick between my shoulder blades that knocked all the wind out of me. I fell like a limp rag. I tried to get oxygen back into my lungs as I tasted the blood that overflowed from my mouth.

Oh my God, I thought. *I'm going to die.* It didn't matter if I'd had a premonition or not. I didn't stand a chance.

"God-damn, bitch," the voice hissed at me.

He grabbed me by my ponytail. He smelled of sweat and stale beer. And in an electrifying second, I knew who it was.

"Finish it, asshole," I said. "But you've never been much of a finisher, have you? He threw his weight on top of me. "I'm going to take care of that now."

He grabbed me around the throat and began to squeeze my windpipe with his thumbs as I struggled for air.

I couldn't hold on much longer. I remember thinking about my aunt, and for a minute I thought I could see Hugh's spirit. But then

I heard the *crack* of a gunshot, and in a split second I found myself gasping for air and sucking in oxygen again.

With all my remaining strength, I pushed my husband's dead body off me with distaste. The body fell to the floor with a *thud*. I stared at a bullet hole drilled precisely through the middle of his forehead.

In shock, I started to shake.

I remember the sound of the siren in the distance. Everything hurt, but it didn't hurt. I guessed that was the shock, too. *Or it's the damage he's done to my physical body?* It was like an out-of-body experience—the ambulance—Verde Valley Medical Center—lights—and then dark.

I woke up when I thought I heard my former nurse again. I figured I must be in hell and that this was karmic payback.

"Lizzy," the nurse said as her face hovered over me.

"A crap-ass day," I moaned.

"Feisty," she said to Hall.

He had leaned over to have a closer look at me. "Tell me about it," he said.

Much to my chagrin, my deceased husband spent the last seconds of his life on top of me. He'd never have that position again.

I learned from Hall that as I was squish-kebabbed by my husband, his hands around my throat in a chokehold, a precise shot killed him. And while that was the official police report offered by the Sedona Police Department, I didn't completely understand it. I'd been there. To get a shot off like that through the window was not the standard. Not even close. It would take someone with remarkable sharpshooting skills to take a shot like that with success.

My nurse left to administer to another patient, and I confronted John Hall.

"That was a one-in-a-million shot."

"I was lucky, I guess," he said.

"You're not a very good liar, Hall."

He pretended to look hurt. He was dressed in khaki pants that were tight in a good way.

"Probably a military sharpshooter could have made that shot at that angle," I said.

"I think," Officer J. Hall said, "that you're suffering from post-traumatic shock. The report stands. It was a lucky shot."

"And I think," I said, "that you're Huckleberry Finn."

The nurse came back through the door with an air of authority and an upturned smile on the corner of her mouth. "Okay, you two, enough for tonight. You need some sleep," she said to me.

I felt like I'd been run over by a truck.

I had stitches on my right arm from the broken glass, and I didn't even want to know what my face looked like. But I sure as hell looked a lot better than my husband did.

Good news came from Uncle Callaghan. "Your husband died before any divorce decree was signed," he said, "so you're a widow. We'll argue that the property and assets are all yours. Since Mr. O'Brien is your attorney of record, he will assist with the probate."

Chapter 27
Blessings and Parting

REBECCA PICKED ME UP IN her BMW from the Verde Valley Medical Center when I'd been discharged.

"Feel up for a ride?" Rebecca asked after I'd put on my seat belt.

"Absolutely," I answered.

She accelerated and headed south.

"You have most of this figured out?" I asked Rebecca as I drank in the fresh air. It was a relief not to smell hospital-strength antiseptic.

"I think," Rebecca said, "your husband came to Sedona to kill you. I'm sorry I suggested you should be nice to him."

"And he was almost successful," I added. "Where are we going?"

"People have asked about you. We're meeting them at the Crystal Grotto."

The light was lovely in the inner grotto. "You knew," I said to Kuruk, and I went over to shake his hand.

"Spirit knew," he answered.

We were at Enchantment Resort in Boynton Canyon, and I could feel the energy of the Kachina Vortex behind us. At Miiamo, next to the vortex, is a room called the Crystal Grotto. Rebecca and I sat in a circle, the circle of life represented in the shape of the room. In the ceiling is a skylight that directs the sun's rays toward a piece of granite—a high-energy vibration—that gushes with water through the center and pools out below it. The ground is sand. At the summer solstice, the sun enters the skylight and the sun's rays fall directly over the center of the granite.

I was there, with Kuruk, and Lynea, and Rebecca. We'd joined in the circle for the blessing and the Navajo travel song.

Kuruk used a pipe to call Spirit and took an eagle feather and dipped it in the water as it bubbled up through a crack in the granite crystal. He shook the feather over us and blessed us. We breathed deeply the sage-scented air, and he blessed us. He ended with a Navajo song to guard me in my travels.

After Kuruk finished, I walked through the doorway of the Crystal Grotto with a feeling that things had aligned in my world. But I still needed to say a final goodbye before I left.

When I walked out of the Miiamo, I looked up at the Kachina Woman Vortex and watched the light play upon the red rocks.

It's hard to say goodbye to something that you're not quite ready to let go of. As I looked up toward the Kachina, I saw Danny's silhouette.

I headed up the trail. When I got to the plateau of the vortex, I looked around, but I couldn't see him. That's when I heard the haunting melody of the native flute. Following the sound, I couldn't see anything, but I stopped, closed my eyes, and listened as the last notes dissipated into the red rocks. I felt the familiar tingling sensation from the ground into my feet, and up to the top of my ankles. I opened my eyes. Danny was in front of me. His raven hair was blown by the wind.

"I'm here to make amends," I said.

I had no business being angry at Danny. He'd saved my life twice. He didn't owe me anything; he didn't promise me anything. It was what I projected on him that I wanted, but that was my problem, not his. And without him, I would be dead.

"Thank you," I said, "for the shot that saved my life."

He came over and embraced me.

And that was almost the last time I saw Danny.

Chapter 28
The Gray-White Owl

I HAD A FEW MORE pieces of background to finish painting before I could leave Ryan to his next season of the theater. I had the intent of putting the finishing strokes on the woodland set backgrounds tonight. I'd mixed the paints and had the palette of colors in front of me. The next play—*A Midsummer Night's Dream*—is the story of love out of balance and love regaining balance once again.

I heard some commotion outside, so I stopped and placed my brush on my palette. I was close to finishing. When I opened the door, the sun was down and the early-evening light fell upon the fountain in the courtyard. I saw something that made me look again. Beside the fountain was a gray-white owl. It turned toward me. The owl in the spirit world is the messenger of clairvoyance or insight. It is the totem of psychics and clairvoyants. It was the owl that came to me in the desert when I was lost.

"Aunt Thelma," I said, "you've come to say goodbye."

I went back inside and put the last strokes of paint on the fairy-forest background. I signed the bottom and dated it, and I cleaned up the paints.

On the way to the parking lot, I passed the jewelry store that sold the sapphire ring. I decided to take one last look at it. The salesman recognized me; however, he was ready to close for the evening.

"Still open?" I asked.

"Take your time," he said.

I went over to the case with the sapphire ring.

He walked over and stood behind it. "It's interesting," he said, "the way a piece of jewelry asks someone to own it."

An aura emanated from it. He unlocked the case and set the ring on a piece of black velvet. I watched as colors emerged from the stone, its own geometry of energy radiating from it.

"Sapphire is the stone of wisdom. The blue sapphire connects to the wearer and keeps her on a spiritual path," he said. "You have an interesting aura yourself."

"You see mine?"

"Yes."

"My aunt was clairvoyant. She could read auras."

"She's with you now."

I knew that was true.

"Tell you what," he said as I handed the ring back to him, "I'll give you a discount."

In the past if someone said something like that to me, I would have thought that it was part of the psychology of the sale. *What is it about jewelry and me?* I regarded it as a poultice of sorts. But maybe it wasn't the shopping after all—maybe there was a mystical pull toward certain objects.

"I can't afford it," I said as I looked at the ring one last time. "I'm in financial limbo right now."

"I'll sell it to you at my cost," he said as he wrote down the figure on a piece of paper.

I looked at the price. It was discounted well below anything I'd expected.

"Are you going to wear it, or do you want it in a box?"

At that point I did something I'd never been able to do before. "No, thank you," I said as I turned and left the store.

Chapter 29
Closing Curtain

ATTORNEY O'BRIEN LEFT A MESSAGE at my apartment on my telephone answering machine. I knew it was too late to reach him, but I called back anyway. I left a message and was surprised when he picked up the telephone.

"The last will and testament of your husband looks in order. You're the beneficiary. I've prepared the papers for the probate matter, and I don't anticipate a problem. I'll need your signature on some of the paperwork. When do you plan to arrive in Portland?"

"I leave tomorrow."

The next message didn't surprise me. But it was still hard to hear. The assisted living center called and left a message about my aunt's passing.

Of course, I knew she had gone to the other side.

I called and said that I would be in Portland within three days to make the funeral arrangements.

I listened to the last message. It was a dinner invitation from John Hall. I called him back.

"Will you come to dinner?" he asked. I debated the merits of another dinner with John Hall. He must have sensed my hedge. "Please," he added.

"If you want to pick up some Chinese food," I said, "we can eat it at my place. I'll unpack a few plates. I'm leaving tomorrow and still have a lot of work to do." I needed to load all my boxes into the U-Haul trailer I'd rented. I planned to coax the Subaru through the desert.

I went through and cleaned each room. It was a systemic approach, and I wanted to get some of my cleaning deposit back. I lost track of time. When Hall came to the door with the food, I was dirty and sweaty. He smelled like fresh soap and aftershave.

The contrast between the two of us couldn't have been greater.

I cleared off a section of the kitchen table and was ready to unpack two plates and forks when Hall unpacked two of everything that he'd brought and pulled out ice cold beers. I sat down in the kitchen chair with a sigh and took the cold bottle to my forehead.

We loaded our plates with Kung Pao chicken, Yang Chow fried rice, egg rolls, crispy green beans—deep fried, and when dipped in the special sauce, addicting.

We were in the midst of seconds when I heard a knock at the door. Karma had curled herself into a ball and fallen asleep on Hall's feet.

"Hi," Rebecca said at my doorstep, "I thought I would come by and say goodbye."

I invited her inside and offered her some Chinese food. She looked between Hall and me and said, "Bad timing."

"Not at all," I said and unpacked one of my plates and a fork and filled her plate. I found a spare chair and pulled it to the table.

"The food comes with a price. We could use some help taking these boxes out to the U-Haul after we eat," I said.

Hall reached down and petted Karma.

"We got to know each other that night you were in the medical center," he said. "I thought I'd just run in and take her out and feed her like we'd planned. But Karma had a different idea," he added. "She didn't respond the night your husband attacked you. She knew him, I guess, so she didn't maintain a protective stance."

I thought back to better times when we'd worked on our house in Portland—when everything still seemed possible. But under the semblance of normalcy were the dark secrets of my husband's life, and I shuddered to think about how I'd been duped.

Rebecca read both my mood and my mind. "Love is blind," she said.

Oh, it is, I thought. *Very blind.*

"I figured out that your husband thought he could get everything if you were dead," Rebecca said. "He found someone to do it, but what he didn't anticipate was the total ineptness of the people he'd contracted."

"That," Hall said, "and the fact that there was someone else in Sedona—also working at the theater—who looked a lot like you. I think it confused things for awhile and bought you a little time."

I thought back to how much Nicole and I did look alike. It was a topic of conversation when I'd worked with her at the theater in Oregon. Even Dave Lewis had asked me if we had met before. I had forgotten about our similar appearances since we were so different on the personality front.

"I think when the opportunity and means presented itself," Rebecca said, "they killed Nicole. Unfortunately, Hugh was collateral damage."

Hall cleared his throat. I'd almost forgotten that he was there. He had listened to our amateur conjecture. "I was going to tell you tonight about the newest development in the case," he said.

Rebecca and I hung onto our chairs for whatever it was that could be new information. "Dave Lewis and his friend were about to be arrested this morning close to the United States and Mexican border. They were in a rental car and attempted to get to the other side. But they didn't make it," he said.

"Are they going to be brought back here for arraignment?" I asked.

"No," he said, "but they will be back for a funeral."

"What happened?" I asked with a gasp.

"When the border patrol stopped the car and searched it, they found it loaded with drugs. They resisted arrest, ran, and were killed."

"So we'll never know for sure what the connection was between them?"

"Not for sure. But based on your husband's work with the Portland police and his involvement with prostitutes, I'm certain there's a connection."

It's hard to know you've been married to a cheater. It's even harder to find out that someone you loved planned to kill you.

"Well," I said, ready to dismiss the somber tone the evening had taken, "I am very grateful for your help."

We spent the better part of the next couple of hours loading boxes into the U-Haul.

Rebecca asked, "Are you ready to pack your aunt's books yet?"

"She died yesterday," I said.

"Oh my gosh," Rebecca said, "I'm so sorry. I had no idea."

Hall came over and put his arm around me. I knew he was looking for an excuse to do that.

"I knew it before I got the call," I said. "I was at the theater working on the final background for next season's play, and something made me look outside. I went out, and perched on the courtyard fountain was gray-white owl. It was like the one I saw when I was lost in the desert. But this time I knew something was different. This time I knew my aunt had passed. And then when I went into the jewelry store—"

Rebecca interrupted me. "You got the ring!"

"No," I said. "That was unusual, too, because for the first time that I can remember, I didn't need to have it."

"I think you've had a spiritual paradigm shift."

"I think I've figured out some of the patterns I need to acknowledge," I said as I looked at Hall. "And I'm by no means perfect," I added.

Rebecca looked between the two of us. "Time for me to go. I'll let you two pack the books." She came over to me, and we hugged each other. "Thank you," she said, "for everything."

"And thank you," I said. "I'll be in touch when I visit you in New York."

I didn't tell her about the cute NYC boyfriend I'd seen for her. She'd be able to figure that out herself.

She looked at me and was ready to ask a question, but she decided to let it drop.

After she left, Hall pulled out some chocolate truffles, so we ate them and I poured a little bit of wine I still had left in my refrigerator. We went out by the pool and watched the stars for a short break. I was getting stiff from all the packing, and the wine was beginning to make me sleepy. But sometimes when you know you're not going to be someplace or with someone for long, there's an ache to savor the moment and commit it to memory. Later on, you can go back to those moments and relive them—a time capsule of life.

I pulled my sweater around me.

Hall asked the question that hung in the air: "Do you think we'll see each other again?"

"Well," I said, "I don't know."

"Okay," he said, "I don't like that answer, so now I'd like one a little more encouraging."

"So," I began, "you want a reading—even though you know it's an undeveloped talent."

"Tell me my future."

We turned the chairs toward each other, and I had him hold out his hands toward mine. While I looked at him, I saw an expansion of light.

"You're colorful," I said.

"What's that mean?" he asked.

"I have no idea," I said. "Let's go check and see if there's anything in my aunt's books." The lights from the apartment glowed yellow. I looked through several of them, but I didn't find anything helpful about auras. I tried to remember my aunt and her readings. "I think my aunt used tea leaves and vibrations from objects and those kinds of things for readings," I said. "I'm not getting anything here."

Frustrated, Hall took me in his arms and kissed me. And this time, not only did I feel like I was a Hersey's chocolate ready to melt, I realized I'd go to my grave remembering that kiss.

I then considered whether I could remain standing after it.

I couldn't.

The next morning, I woke up to light streaming into my bedroom window. I didn't know where I was for a second and had to orient myself to the day and time. The alarm clock helped with the time part—the numerals read eight o'clock. I was supposed to wake up early to get going for a long day of driving. As I rolled over, I remembered that I'd had a lot more wine, and I also had a faint recollection that I hadn't been alone last night.

I heard a noise in the apartment, and Karma didn't even bother to lift her head. Officer J. Hall came in with two cups of coffee, breakfast rolls, and a big smile on his face.

I've done it again, I thought. All it took was those attractive blue eyes, and—I remembered now—the amazing kisses. It was all coming back to me. Oh, the best-laid plans of mice and men.

Maybe I was being too hard on myself.

He climbed into bed with me and handed me a cup of coffee. It was French roast.

"Wow," I said as I took a big sip. "This tastes great."

We sat up in bed and drank coffee and didn't say anything. He smoothed my morning hair.

When I got out of the shower, he was gone. One box remained to be packed. I wasn't sure why I'd procrastinated on this final box, but it occurred to me that maybe it wasn't that there was some kind of message in the books or some kind of clue. Maybe the books were Aunt Thelma's way of letting me know that we'd always share a special kind of connection to each other. I put packing tape around the box and carried it out to the U-Haul. One more time I went inside and looked around the apartment for anything I might have missed. I let Karma pee, and then she jumped into the back of the Subaru. I cracked the windows for her and walked to the apartment door of the manager. I gave him the key and told him I'd cleaned the apartment and the furniture that was there was left in good condition. He asked where he could send the deposit check. That was a good question. Since I didn't really have any idea where I'd be staying, I gave him the address of my attorney. We said goodbye to each other, and I got into the car to drive. I had some stops to make before I could get on the road.

My first stop was the theater. I clipped on Karma's leash and we walked over together. As I was ready to walk into the green-house office, Ryan came out and so did the rest of the cast. They made me cover my eyes before I could go inside—Simon took Karma's leash—and when they pulled off my blindfold, there was a cake with ice cream and champagne. I went easy on the champagne because I had a long trip ahead of me, but I loaded up on the cake and ice cream. Kayla glowed. I looked at her and the picket fence with the kids flashed in front of me again. That's when I knew. When no one else was too close by, I told her congratulations. She looked at me, surprised at first, and then asked how I knew she was pregnant since she'd just only learned last night when she and her boyfriend took the at-home test.

"I'm psychic," I said with a smile. "And it seems to be growing," I added.

She hugged me. "We're so excited."

"I'll be back for the wedding," I said.

"You knew we'd get married."

"That night in my apartment," I said, "I had a clear vision. But since I hadn't had anything like that before, I wasn't confident enough to tell you. Especially if I got it wrong."

I decided it really wasn't any of my business to tell her about the other three children she would have since she hadn't asked.

Simon and the rest of the crew came and offered one last good-bye. Ryan handed me my final paycheck which I knew I'd need to tide me over until I got the rest of the accounts in order with Jake O'Brien's help. He told me there was a little extra in there for all my help.

That's when he handed me a box with a blue ribbon on it. I told him he shouldn't have done anything else. He told me he hadn't.

"Who did?" I asked.

"That policeman came by and told me to give it to you."

I opened the box and inside was the blue sapphire ring set in white gold.

I was speechless. And that doesn't happen very often.

John Hall knew that I would never have accepted the ring this morning in my apartment. I would have insisted he take it back.

I gave everyone a final hug and walked over the cobblestones to Soul Creations. The same clerk was in the shop. He turned his angular features toward me as I came inside. I had the ring on my right hand, where it fit perfectly. There was no need to size it.

"So, the ring found its owner," the clerk said with a smile.

"When did he come in and buy it?" I asked.

"About an hour ago."

He bought it after I told him we might not see each other again, I thought.

"Did he get the discount?"

"Of course," he said. "I knew it was going to you. I felt it the first time you were in the store and he was behind you."

"You're psychic?" I asked.

"You don't have to be psychic to see someone in love," he said. "And he, my friend, *is* in love with you."

I'm not good at love, I thought. *I'm not good at relationships. I don't get involved with men who are emotionally available, and the ones who are, that are attracted to me, I can't see in front of my own face. I have some kind of psychic ability, but when it comes to love, I'm blind.*

My last stop was to see Peace. She had a sign on the storefront door that she was closed for an hour. She was out gathering some medicinal herbs while she was living her past soul life as an alchemist.

I was disappointed that I wasn't going to be able to say goodbye to her personally when I saw an Alien Recovery Team Car pull into the parking lot. Out stepped Peace.

"I had to get back to say goodbye," she said to me as she came over and hugged me. "The alien portal opened, and they communicated with me that you were leaving."

I sat down, this time in the back of her shop, with a cup of green tea that she'd brewed for me. "It's only green tea," she said with her trademark laugh. "You've got a long road ahead of you."

"Well…" I began.

"Well, nothing," she said as she read my mind. "Ask the question that you want the answer to."

"Okay," I said, "how did the Chevy explode that was chasing me? I should have been dead. But I also remember that I heard a noise."

"Now," she said, "we're down to business." She leaned in closer. "I'll tell you everything in all seriousness. Are you ready?"

I claimed that I was. I didn't expect what I got.

"A portal opened to the alien world. I communicated with them…"

Oh boy, I thought.

"Come on, hear me out," she said.

"I will attempt to remain open."

"Good," she said, "because now comes the military part. Do you know that the military is housed under the Enchantment Resort at Boynton Canyon? Many people hike the trail at the Kachina Woman Vortex and escape all sense of time—even go missing for hours and hours—though it is a very short hike. Many people experience the sound of footsteps, but no one ever appears. People take photographs of deer on the trail, but when looking at the photograph, a ghostly image is there instead. Some hikers report seeing a black helicopter when on the trail to Kachina Woman, and they often see men in military clothing."

"I didn't see anything like that when I was there."

"That's because you weren't meant to see it."

"So what does this have to do with me and the Chevy?"

"I was getting to that."

She filled up my cup with more hot water and packed more tea leaves to make another cup.

"Let's get back to the military. It's believed they have a complex under the Enchantment Resort. The military bought the resort and now it acts as a cover. All of this is on the Internet. The military purchased the resort because they recognize the energy of the vortex. It's not only eons of Indian tribes that recognize that it is something from out of this world."

Peace paused to sip her tea. "So, I used my UFO and military connections," she added.

"And how did you know I needed help?"

"I'm psychic, remember."

"You read minds, and you're psychic, and you see UFOs?"

"Correct."

"Peace, let's say for the sake of argument that you did know that I was in danger and needed help. And let's also say, for the sake of argument, that you used your UFO and military connections. So how did that car catch fire? Because all I saw was smoke."

"Military drones. Those small, unmanned planes they use."

"So are you telling me that a military drone fired on the Chevy?"

"Well," Peace said, "let's call it a timely military test on a test target."

I liked it better when I thought it was the aliens. I gave up on getting any further explanation from Peace. Something made me realize that while she was spinning a tale about aliens and portals and the military, there was some truth somewhere. *Is she military?* And the fact that her name was Peace—the antitheses of war—made me think it even more likely. *Or is she certifiably crazy?*

Finally, I was on the road. Karma was in the backseat, and I was making pretty good time. It was a clear and sunny day. The radio was turned off. I was close to the reservation, headed north, when I thought I heard an Indian flute. In the middle of nowhere, I saw a lone Navajo at a stand by the side of the road, selling souvenirs.

On an impulse, I pulled over. Puffs of red-rock dust came out from under my feet as I walked over and greeted him.

"Do you get many customers out here?" I asked.

"Not too many," he answered.

He picked up a flute and began to play. As I listened, I thought I heard three flutes.

"Is that a travel blessing song?" I asked.

"Yes," he said. "It's a special request."

"Who requested it?"

Without a word, the Navajo pointed up to the red-rock rim of the butte, and I thought I saw, or at least I believe I saw, Kuruk and Danny standing side by side, flutes in hand, waving goodbye.

Acknowledgments

Thank you to R. J. Joseph, Loretta Barrett Oden, David Begay, and Bob Bear for the talking circle, travel songs, sacred medicine, stories, and blessings.

About the Author

A NATIVE OREGONIAN, KELLY RUNNING coaxes an appreciation for the English language into irrepressible seventh and eighth graders. Her poetry and essays appear in prestigious West Coast journals. Earlier in her career, she wrote commercials and press releases for radio. Her passion for research and interest in indigenous spiritualism instills authenticity in her storytelling. www.kellyrunningmysteries.com.

www.ingramcontent.com/pod-product-compliance
Lightning Source LLC
Chambersburg PA
CBHW071207260626
47162CB00004B/1198